KJ CHARLES

First published by Samhain Publishing. This revised edition published 2017.

Published by KJC Books

Cover design by Lexiconic Design
Interior design by eB Format
Swirl created by Alvaro_cabrera - Freepik.com
Edited by Anne Scott

Print ISBN: 978-1-9997846-4-5

To Ted with all my love

CHAPTER ONE

Ben hated London.

He hated the shouting, the crowded streets, the smell. He hated the pinch-faced beggars, the flower girls with their paltry, wilted offerings, and the frock-coated men who strode busily by. He hated Lincoln's Inn Fields, a pleasant garden square ringed with trees in the heart of the greatest city in the world. He hated the early blossom on those trees, hated it with a savage, glowering passion, as though it had done him a personal injury. He hated, more than anything else, the bitter misery that hung around him in a cloud that blotted out the springtime sun.

If he had smiled in the last few months, he could not remember the occasion. He didn't suppose he was likely to smile again soon even if he achieved his aim here, but by God, he would wipe the smile off another face, and perhaps then the poisonous knot in his chest would loosen at last. Perhaps.

His destination was on the corner of Lincoln's Inn Fields and Sardinia Street, an unimpressive red-brick building that gave no hint of its purpose in its appearance. The large wooden doors were locked. Ben knocked, a bit too loudly. The doorman who answered was sturdy, keen-eyed and unwelcoming.

"Yes?"

"Constable Marshall, Hertfordshire constabulary. I have an appointment with Mr. Peter Janossi."

"Can you prove that?" asked the doorman.

Ben pulled out the letter from Janossi, a brief note simply setting their meeting time and this address. The paper was not of notable quality and bore a rather undistinguished crest, with no other heading.

"Wait here." The doorman took it and retreated into the building, shutting the door. Ben waited. He had no other options.

It was a good five minutes standing on the step before the doors were opened again. Their guardian beckoned him in.

"All right, Constable, you can go through. Mr. Waterford, show him to Mr. Janossi, would you?"

The words were addressed to a pudgy young man with possibly the most badly broken nose Ben had ever seen, and as a once-keen rugby player, he had seen a lot of them. Waterford looked like he'd been kicked in the face by a mule. He gave the doorman a resentful glance and slouched off through the hallway, Ben following.

The hall was large and high-ceilinged, a little grander than the outside of the building suggested. It was hung with heavy, gilt-framed oil paintings, radiating wealth and history and privilege that made Ben bristle with instant dislike. These people were privileged all right, privileged in a way that was so unfair and unquestionable that his fists clenched.

His guide paused at a grand set of mahogany doors, firmly shut, to exchange a low word with a harried-looking man who waited outside, holding a large leather bag at arm's length. It reeked of spice. Ben waited, staring at an engraving on the wall. It showed some vicious-looking aristocratic swine with a face that begged to have the sneer knocked off it, seated at a desk with a magpie in front of him.

Ben did not want to be here. Not in this building, not with these people, nowhere near. But it was far too late to run now, so instead he wished that the mannerless oaf would stop wasting his damned time and let him get on. He wished that he didn't need to do this, that he had help, that he wasn't alone.

Waterford was still talking. Ben waited politely for a few moments, then abandoned that to stare openly at the man. It had no effect. At last Waterford finished his conversation and jerked his head at Ben. "Well, come on. Mustn't keep the *justiciary* waiting." He loaded the word with dislike. The harried man rolled his eyes.

Ben followed as Waterford led him to a back corridor lined with much less impressive doors, and threw one open without knocking. "Hertfordshire police," he snapped, turned on his heel and stalked off. Ben glanced after him, then looked into the room. A young man sat at the desk, glaring in the direction Waterford had taken.

"Peter Janossi?" Ben asked.

"Oh. Yes. And you're the man from Hertfordshire, Constable, uh." He waved his hand to indicate that his visitor's name was on the tip of his tongue, and in no way forgotten. Ben didn't help him. "Come in. Sit. That is…"

There was no seat. Every available surface was covered with piles of paper, dockets, files, and…*things*, bits of wood and metal, tiny bottles, what looked like a fur stole, and something like a broken umbrella made of leather. Janossi hauled himself to his feet with a grunt, picked this up with two fingertips and turfed it into a corner, onto a teetering stack of books and papers, revealing a chair.

"Sit," he repeated, with some satisfaction, returning to his own chair. "Good morning."

Ben sat, assessing the man. Janossi was a well-built, square-jawed fellow in his midtwenties, a little shorter than his own five foot ten, with light brown hair and vivid green eyes. He looked tired and somewhat beleaguered. He didn't look special, or gifted, or strange, or magical.

"Right, Constable, uh…Constable. You got here, then. Sorry about Waterford." Janossi made a face to indicate his opinion of Ben's guide, and began to scrabble through one of the piles of paper on his desk. "So, you wrote me a letter, which, uh…letter, letter…" He plucked out a paper and scanned it quickly. "Right, yes of course, Constable Marshall. You've come about Jonah Pastern." He frowned. "You're from the Hertfordshire constabulary. The police force. Not the justiciary?"

"No. I worked with the justiciary on his case." The word came out so easily now, considering how shocking it had been to learn it just a few months ago. The justiciary. Secret policemen, bringing law to secret people.

"Right, yes, yes. Hertfordshire. You were the people who let him go."

Ben's jaw tightened. "He escaped."

"Yes, well, he does that." Janossi's frown deepened. He put the paper down. "Constable, are you working with the Metropolitan Police on this?"

"No," Ben admitted, with reluctance. This was one of the sticking points he'd feared. If the London justiciary simply directed him to the Met, this whole thing would be a waste of time. As if his time could be wasted. "I'm here on behalf of Hertfordshire. We lost him, we'd like to find him."

Janossi blinked. "You're trying to pick Pastern up because he escaped from custody?"

"Yes." Obviously. As he'd written.

"Because he escaped *last October*?"

"Yes, last October. He's still missing and we still want him back."

Janossi's face had settled into what looked like a habitual scowl. "Do you even know what happened this winter?"

Ben gritted his teeth. "If there's something I should know, Mr. Janossi, please tell me."

"Pastern? The Met? Dead policemen? You don't know, do you? For God's sake." Janossi sounded utterly exasperated. "I'd have thought it might have occurred to *somebody* to put the word out."

Ben bit back the urge to shout at him. "What, exactly, are you talking about?"

"Oh Lord." Janossi sat back, shoulders dropping. "We had a problem here, Constable. A criminal gang, made up of practitioners. You know what that means?"

"Magicians." He'd seen it, seen them at work, but the word still sounded extraordinary. "People who can do...*things*."

"We have certain powers, yes." Janossi looked rather uncomfortable. "Anyway there were four of them. Jonah Pastern was one."

"Pastern in a gang," Ben repeated. "Of thieves?"

"Oh, thieves would have been marvellous." Janossi made a face. "No. They had...complicated aims." He waved a hand. "Doesn't matter now. It's been dealt with. But on the way, they killed—murdered—four police officers. Two retired, two serving."

Ben swallowed, trying to keep the movement unobtrusive, but his throat had tightened to the point that it felt difficult to breathe. "Four officers."

"One of them was the officer who liaised with the justiciary. Inspector Rickaby, he was called. They ripped him in half, tore his head open. We couldn't let his wife and children see the body."

Ben stared at the man. "*How?*"

"Practitioners can do things like that. That's why we have the justiciary, to try and stop them." Janossi grimaced at Ben's expression. "It was an appalling business, and the Met are—well, *angry* doesn't begin to describe it. Four murdered coppers, and nobody even arrested for it, let alone convicted."

"The gang got away?" Ben asked. He was distantly surprised by the steadiness of his own voice.

"Pastern got away. The other three died, which was the best thing for it, but the Met weren't happy. They want a culprit, someone to stand trial for murder. That's Pastern or no one, now."

Murder. Jonah Pastern, a murderer.

"Why haven't you got him then?" Ben asked. "Four police officers—why's he still at large?" He welcomed the anger that rose through him. "Why hasn't he been caught yet? Why aren't you going after him?"

"Yes, well, it's not quite that easy. For one thing, we don't know where he is, and for another—do you know what he can do?"

"He walks on the air," Ben said. "I saw him do it."

"Saw him, and lost him. You'll know as well as we do how hard it is to keep hold of the swine. We've a windwalker of our own on the justiciary, which should give us a chance of catching him if we find him, but we can't just keep her hanging around on rooftops, when for all anyone knows Pastern's in Glasgow or Dover or Constantinople." Janossi shrugged. "We're under pressure here, Constable. Not enough experienced justiciars, one of our most senior people off active duty and another retiring next month. We don't have the manpower to go hunting Pastern, and that's all there is to it. If you want to assist the Met, or look for him at your own risk, be my guest. If you find him, let me know, and we'll come and get him for you. But I'll tell you now, if we do that, we'll give him to the Met, not back to Herts. Dead policemen outweigh an escape from custody."

"Good. He can go to the Met, and the gallows. He deserves it." Ben's voice didn't sound quite like his own, but there was no doubt in his heart. There was nothing in his heart but dull, scouring disgust. Nothing at all.

"It's a bit more complicated than that, I'm afraid," Janossi said. "I didn't work on the case myself, but as I recall— Oh, just a minute, there's Mrs. Gold. She'll know. Mrs. Gold! Do you have a moment?"

Ben twisted round at Janossi's cry. He was sure he'd shut the door behind him, and it was indeed closed. There was no aperture or window in the door to see through, but as he looked, it opened, and a dark-haired woman in an advanced state of pregnancy plodded in, heavy-footed. Ben leapt up with automatic courtesy. The woman didn't seem to notice him.

"You called, Joss?"

"Can I have a minute? It's about Jonah Pastern."

Mrs. Gold made a face of loathing and took the chair, seating herself with heavy care. Ben hovered awkwardly.

"This is Constable, um, from Hertfordshire," Janossi said. "He worked with Miss Nodder's justiciary up there, on Pastern."

Mrs. Gold cocked her head to look up. "Oh, yes. You were the people who lost him in that farcical manner. Thank you so much. We had the obnoxious little gadfly making bad worse all through December because of that. I hope you're here to redeem your force's blunder."

Ben hadn't had a woman speak to him like that since he'd left dame school. He had no idea what to say to that chilly voice, but apparently his spine knew exactly how to react, because he found he was standing very straight, head up and staring ahead.

She didn't seem to expect a reply, turning back to Janossi. "What about Pastern?"

"Well, I haven't really looked into the case. I did know the constable was coming, but the files are somewhere in Mr. Day's office, probably, and—"

"Say no more," Mrs. Gold told him. "When we bid farewell to Steph, I'm going to throw a lighted match in there and seal the door. I might not even wait for him to leave. What do you need to know?"

"Where to start looking for him," Ben said.

"How dangerous he is," Janossi added. "And what his role was in that business. It wasn't him who killed the policemen, was it?"

Mrs. Gold glanced between the two men, considering. "In reverse order. Pastern was a minor part of a major conspiracy. He committed a series of thefts and deliberately implicated an innocent woman, and he was accessory to murder. How dangerous he is…I don't know. He seems to be quite without morals, and I shouldn't wish to see an innocent standing between him and something he wanted. Are you all right, Constable?"

Her dark eyes were locked on Ben's, her nose flaring slightly in concentration. He swallowed. "Yes, ma'am. Go on."

"Where to look. Well, if I knew that, I'd go and get him myself. Not *myself*, Joss," she added impatiently, as Janossi's mouth opened. "I would tell *you* to do it, because I'm only allowed to waddle the corridors like an overstuffed goose, poking my beak into things."

"Three more months," Janossi murmured, voice soothing.

Ben blinked at that—the woman looked huge to his inexpert eye. He didn't think he'd done anything but blink, but she glanced up at him, and said, "Twins. Anyway. We have no idea if Pastern's still in London, but if he is, where I would look, if I was allowed to do anything and if we weren't overstretched to the point of madness, and if I felt he wouldn't simply flee on sight, is places like Holywell Street, Piccadilly, Cleveland Street. The men's meeting places."

Ben was no expert on London, but he knew what that litany of names meant, and he could feel the colour heating his face. Janossi had also gone red. Mrs. Gold looked between them, unembarrassed. "Well, that's one thing we know about Pastern for certain, he's that way. Enthusiastically, I'm told. Isn't that how he got away from your lot, Constable? Seduced the arresting officer?"

Janossi gave a crack of laughter. Ben managed a stiff nod.

"So I'd start in those places, for lack of anywhere else. But as I said, I can't guarantee he's still in London at all, and if he is, he's lying low. If you do find him, Constable, don't try to take him in yourself. He's reckless, reasonably powerful, and very slippery. I'd give you someone to work with, but we don't have anyone to spare."

"If we get him, what will we do?" Janossi asked her. "No point handing him to the Met if he gets away five minutes later. That'll just irritate them."

"Windwalkers." Mrs. Gold pulled a face. "He'll have to be hobbled. I expect we'll cut the tendons in his calves. It's about the only way to bring his sort down to earth."

Janossi grimaced. "Saint won't like that."

"Yes, she will," Mrs. Gold said. "Or perhaps she won't, but she's leaving us along with Steph, so be damned to her opinion. Good luck, Constable. Joss will make a list of places you can try looking. If you should snout anything out, come back to us rather than the Met, and we might even give you a fighting chance."

Ben left Janossi and the Council not long afterwards. He had never wanted to leave a place so much. His head was throbbing with all he'd learned. He hadn't eaten all day but the thought of food made his stomach roil; he would have liked a pint of ale, or more, but he could not bear to sit. He strode out instead, through the London streets, not knowing or caring where his legs took him.

Jonah, part of a criminal gang. Jonah hobbled, gaoled, unable to walk. Jonah, in some molly club, fucking other men. *Enthusiastically.*

Jonah, accessory to murder.

Bile rose in his throat and he almost retched, holding it back with an effort of will. The taste was sour in his mouth. He'd thought Jonah had stripped him of everything, had thought there was nothing more to lose, but he'd been wrong. There had been a few last precious memories, but they were falling around him in shards now, their painted shell cracking and peeling away to reveal the true rotten nature of the man.

He wanted to scream aloud, or to weep, or to pound his fist into that laughing mouth till it was broken and silenced for good. Treacherous, murderous Jonah had ruined his life, and that left Ben nothing but vengeance.

One year ago

It began in a discreet establishment in St. Albans.

The tiny cathedral city was not a place one might have expected to find a house of ill repute. That was all the better, so far as Ben was concerned. He needed to be far enough from his own town of Berkhamsted that he could feel reasonably sure he would not be recognised; he needed a place where every man present knew what he was after. No misunderstandings that led to cries of outrage and the summoning of the law.

He didn't do this often. Perhaps four times a year, some way from home, with the utmost discretion. Just for the human contact, just for the knowledge that there were other men like him, just for the company.

Not *just* for the company. That was clearly not true.

As it happened, the company that night was poor. The inconspicuous little place was half-empty, and nobody who was there caught his eye in the least. Many of them tried, which would have been flattering in a different crowd. Ben was a powerfully built young man, and his square shoulders and serious expression evidently gave him some sort of appeal, but he was well aware that he had not been blessed with remarkable looks. He was an ordinary sort of fellow, and that was quite all right with him. He wasn't here for much. Faceless fumbles with strangers or quick, shameful, hidden encounters in back alleys. That was what there was for him, and he didn't waste much time bemoaning it. He controlled his appetites, indulged them now and again, arrested people at work, didn't get arrested himself. It was his life, and it worked well enough.

Still, it would have been pleasant to meet someone to share a few words with.

He sighed and sipped his drink in the consciousness of an uninspiring evening to come. He would have another ale, and pick whoever looked the least likely to be poxed, and have his cock sucked in the alley outside, since it would be pointless not to bother having come this far, and that would be that for another few months. It was about as much as he could expect. He would have been a fool if he'd hoped for more.

The door opened. Ben looked up, and the foundations of his life began to crumble.

The man walked in with a light, athletic grace to his movements. He had black hair that looked windswept, and deep cobalt-blue eyes that sparkled like sapphires in the gaslight, and a wide, wicked mouth that seemed poised to smile. He glanced around, one quick, practised sweep of the room, and his gaze found Ben's. Then he was over, pulling up a chair without asking permission, the quick-dawning smile on his lips fulfilling all their promise.

"I'm Jonah," he said. "You look nice."

Ben stared, too amazed to speak. He was vaguely astonished that every other man in the room wasn't staring. He didn't think he could have borne it if Jonah had gone to another table.

Jonah's smile widened. "Do you have a name?"

"Yes," Ben agreed, and a moment later, "That is, it's Ben. Benedict. Ben."

"Ben. Good evening, Ben. I've been looking for you."

"Me?"

Jonah cocked his head to the side, birdlike. "I think so. Don't you?"

"Would you like a drink?" Ben blurted.

"But I don't want you to go all the way to the bar," Jonah pointed out. Ben pushed over his pewter mug without hesitation, and Jonah turned it before he drank, so that his lips rested where Ben's had touched, sharing the ale in a kiss by proxy.

He was sucking Ben in the alley no more than fifteen minutes later. Ben would have done it for him, would have done anything he was asked, but Jonah had gone to his knees without hesitation, those deep eyes sparkling up. His mouth proved as clever and generous as it looked, taking Ben down with gleeful enjoyment. Ben gripped his hair with both hands and came absurdly quickly, so fast that the tremors of pleasure were shot through with both embarrassment at his eagerness and horror that this might be over already. He looked down, appalled at the thought, as Jonah wiped his lips, but the glorious smile held no mockery.

"Did you need that?"

"I needed you," Ben said, surprising himself, and was delighted to see Jonah's smile widen. "Can I…?" He reached out.

Jonah took his hand, rising gracefully from the dusty, dirty ground. "Oh, yes, you *can*. But could we go somewhere more comfortable?"

Then he had Ben by the hand, pulling him along, both of them laughing, even when Jonah had to release him as they came to the street, for the sake of discretion. He followed Jonah, and found himself in a small room in a cheap boarding house that didn't ask questions, and what he'd feared would be a dry, wasted night had been filled with stars.

There was no guilt, no hurry, no shame, nothing rough. Instead it was a whispery, almost giggly exploration of each other, as though they were schoolboys, as though it were the first time. They played each other for hours, taking turns with hands and mouths, stopping to murmur their incredulity at their good fortune: *that you were waiting there, for me. That you came in just then, to me.* That Ben might have gone to another town or Jonah to another pub. They both shuddered at the thought, and laughed because it hadn't happened. And they kissed as well, at absurd length, for minutes at a time. Ben hadn't known much kissing before, hadn't met many men he'd wanted to kiss, but Jonah was made for it. Everything about his mouth was perfect, whether smiling or sucking, kissing or chattering, and Ben lost himself more deeply in wonder every moment.

They lay there till the morning, Ben accepting Jonah's assurance that it was safe here with blithe, unquestioning confidence. Jonah was charmed.

But he had to go at last, as dawn came, back to his duties, and Jonah kissed him goodbye with a cheerful, almost cocky grin. There could be nothing more, Ben knew that, and what they'd shared had been something that he would treasure as a memory through lonely years to come. But he still felt an absurd shiver of pain that Jonah's farewell could be so lighthearted, because somewhere in the depths of his solitude, he had wanted to cry at the parting.

Six days passed. The bittersweet pang of that careless smile didn't fade with time, its bee-sting sharpness always there, tainting the memory of the most joyful night of Ben's life. And then, the next weekend as he patrolled the quiet streets of Berkhamsted, someone fell into step with him.

"Good morning," Jonah said, at his side. "You didn't tell me you were a policeman."

Ben turned and stared, an instinctive fear dawning—blackmail? threats?—but Jonah was smiling, with mischief in his eyes as he murmured, "That explains how you're so good with your truncheon," and Ben found he was smiling unstoppably back.

"What are you doing here?"

"Well, I came to find you, of course." Jonah grinned at him. He was a couple of inches shorter than Ben and only a little less broad, with an acrobat's build, powerful in the shoulders, narrower in the hips, compact muscle worn lightly. He sported a rather dandyish waistcoat of bright pattern, over the chest that Ben had stroked and kissed. The thought of that, the taste of Jonah's skin, came on Ben like a physical touch, and he could barely muster the saliva in his dry mouth to reply.

"Find me?"

"I missed you," Jonah said.

"I missed you," Ben returned, because it was absurdly true.

"I didn't want you to go. I know you had to, but I didn't want you to. So"—Jonah looked uncertain, but his eyes were bright—"I thought I'd come after you."

"How did you know where I was?"

"I went through your pockets." Jonah gave him a blinding smile, and Ben laughed, first because he didn't believe it, and then because Jonah was laughing back at him, and the joy bubbled up like a spring.

After that it was easy. Everything was easy with Jonah.

"I've taken a cottage," he said, naming a little side street off Cross Oak Road. "Very quiet. Two bedrooms. I need a friend to share the costs." It was as simple as that. Ben told his landlady he'd be sharing his friend's expenses, and put his few possessions in a cart, and they were there, together.

CHAPTER TWO

Now

Ben spent a week learning London's meeting-places for men's men. He had no idea if Jonah would frequent these places, if he would prefer the glittering lights of the Alhambra and the Criterion bar, or the smaller, discreet private houses. He was sure Jonah wasn't paying for company. He would be on the trolling grounds of Hyde Park or Piccadilly, meeting or being met, and he would know the sort of place where two fellows could take a room with no questions asked.

All that assuming he was here, and that he hadn't taken another lover, found himself another victim.

Grimly, without pleasure, Ben made himself acquainted with the ways of London's underworld. He began to recognise faces, and attracted some attention himself. It seemed ludicrous: he knew he was nothing out of the ordinary, nothing that a man like Jonah would have looked at twice without an ulterior motive. But evidently something in the line of his mouth and the set of his shoulders made him seem the sort of man who hurt people, and there were men who liked to be hurt. He let a well-dressed dandy suck him in the shadows of Hyde Park one night, and pulled the man's hair till tears came to his eyes because that seemed to be what the fellow wanted. It wasn't what Ben wanted.

"A dark-haired man," he repeated, whenever he judged it right to ask. "Deep blue eyes. Five foot eight. He laughs, all the time. No, I'm not a copper. I just have to find him."

Most of the men he asked weren't helpful. They didn't know Jonah, or if they did they weren't inclined to hand him over to someone with so much roiling anger. He found nothing, and after a week the policemen who patrolled the edges of the dark areas started to recognise him.

That was a problem. The new law meant that he could be arrested on suspicion of soliciting, and gaoled for what the police thought he might do. He had vaguely hoped to obtain some sort of documentation, something he could use to prove his purpose in the search, but he had forgotten to ask Janossi for credentials in his shock at what he'd learned. He could go back, he supposed, or even approach the Met, but it seemed like tempting fate.

He asked a couple of men about discreet houses where one could take rooms for the night. That led to several predictable misunderstandings and some ruffled feathers. It didn't take him anywhere near his quarry.

Nine days after his search began, he saw Jonah in the street.

This was a warm March, but there was still a chill in the air come the evening. Ben was walking up Newman Street as the clocks chimed eight, heading for Cleveland Street. He had been too long in Piccadilly that day, and a policeman had moved towards him. Ben, familiar with the signs of a constable with questions to ask, had ducked into a crowd and made himself scarce, which meant going further afield. He had not wanted to spend any more time in Soho, looking at empty eyes with their febrile glitter of meaningless pleasure in the dark, so he headed up northwards, simply to be somewhere else, and saw him.

The man was several yards ahead, so Ben could only see his back in the crowd, but there was no mistake, no hesitation. Jonah's graceful stroll was embedded in his memory, and Ben's lungs constricted at the sight. For an insane moment he wanted to cry a greeting, to call out, to have Jonah turn and smile and leap into his arms. Then he remembered, and it hurt all over again.

He caught up with rapid, quiet strides. Jonah was in no hurry, it seemed. He didn't look round. Ben wondered what to do—force him into an alley? Accost him in the street? What powers could the man call on?

Jonah crossed the road, turning into Cleveland Street, and headed for Runciman's. Ben had heard of that one. Another of the endless "discreet establishments", it offered drink and like-minded company, and a set of upstairs rooms for those taking advantage of their like minds. Like Jonah, the whore, scratching his itch in some filthy brothel without a thought for the lover he'd destroyed. A man jerked sideways, passing him, and Ben realised he'd snarled aloud.

Jonah was trotting up the steps. Ben followed, tipping the doorman one of his last, precious shillings for the privilege of entry. He couldn't lose Jonah now.

Inside, the evening was only just underway. The room was lit with gas and candles, hung with glittering gilt-framed mirrors. It was all men in here, some in evening dress, a couple in bright uniforms they might or might not have been entitled to wear. And in the middle, Jonah, heading for the bar.

Ben waited while he ordered his drink, watching the barman laugh at something he'd said with what looked like more than professional interest, and stepped forward as Jonah turned, holding a glass of gin. He still wore the remains of his smile to the barman. His gaze fell on Ben, and for a bright, glorious second that smile widened into pure joy. It dropped away as soon as it had come, and Jonah stood with parted lips, quite still.

"Good evening, Jonah." Ben took another step forward.

Jonah's eyes darted from side to side, as though looking for escape. His lips drew into a hesitant smile. "Ben."

He looked different, somehow. Maybe that was because Ben's infatuation was over, or an effect of the light, but he seemed to have lost some of that brilliant sparkle. He seemed tired. And his hair—

"What happened to your hair?" Ben demanded, and cursed himself. Of all the things he'd meant to say, that was not one.

Jonah's hand went up to the thick white streak that zigzagged through his black locks on one side. That had not been there before. "God, isn't it awful." He sounded distracted, like an actor playing the part of Jonah Pastern, and not well. "It wasn't my idea. I had the most appalling winter—"

"No," Ben said. "You didn't."

Jonah stared at him, and Ben could imagine what he saw. The new scar on his temple, a ragged crescent shape scored by broken glass, sewn up with rough stitches. His body marked by hard, forced physical labour, and made leaner by living hand to mouth, husbanding his meagre savings and earnings. His cheap clothing stained by London dust and grime, already worn and fraying thin. The shabby, gaol-marked shadow of a decent man.

Jonah raised the glass of gin to his lips with a hand that shook, and spilled the clear liquor down his chin. He didn't wipe it off. A single viscous droplet hung from the fingers that held the glass, ignored. All the while his deep blue eyes were locked on Ben's gaze.

"Upstairs," Ben told him. "Now."

Jonah put down his glass and went without a word, walking quickly, then almost running, speaking urgently to a doorman who allowed them entrance to the back half of the house, and pointed with a murmur. Ben came after, feeling the blood rising.

Jonah led them up three flights of stairs, into a small room and lit the gas as Ben shut the door. A large metal-framed bed, with a worn sheet spread over it, stains evident in the dim light. A table bearing a ewer, a towel and a half-full bottle of oil. Nothing else but the smell of sweat and semen from previous customers.

Jonah turned to face him, eyes wide and dark in the dim light. "It's not *very* gracious, but—" he began, and Ben punched him in the mouth.

Jonah went down hard, stumbling backwards, and fell onto the bed, clutching his face. Ben was on him at once. He planted his fist in Jonah's stomach, punching down viciously, and as his target doubled over, Ben grabbed his wrist and dragged it to the bedframe. He had been carrying a set of iron cuffs on his belt since he started looking, just for this. He had planned it.

The cuff snapped on to Jonah's wrist, the other clicked over the iron rail of the bedframe, and that was him caught.

Jonah looked up, gasping for breath, mouth wet and red and open, making no effort to move or fight. He was sprawled half on the bed, knees on the floor, and Ben stood over him, and felt the slow burn of something dark and needy rise within.

"You shit. You bastard. But I've got you now."

"Ben." Jonah's tongue darted over his split lip. "Please."

"Please what? Please *what?*" Ben's fingers were clenching. "You destroyed me. You ruined me. I did ten weeks, you fucking coward, while you ran away."

"Oh God." It was a whimper. "I'm sorry, I'm so sorry."

"Ten weeks' gaol, with hard labour. Dishonourably discharged from the force. My parents—" He bent and grabbed Jonah's collar, twisting the cloth tight as he pulled the man up by the neck. "I'm going to make you pay for what you did, you treacherous shit. Give you to the Met, watch them hobble you and gaol you. I hope every minute you serve is as bad as my time was. Oh, but you're a murderer now, aren't you? I hope you hang."

Jonah wheezed, trying to speak, turning red. Ben let go, and he thumped back on the bed, sucking in air. "Not," he managed. "I didn't kill anyone, I swear."

"Shut up. I don't care. No more lies."

Jonah swallowed. "Ben—"

"Shut up!"

He had dreamed of this moment so often, Jonah as helpless as he had made Ben, getting his just deserts at last. He'd imagined beating the man to a pulp, seeing him crying and pleading, his own satisfaction as he redressed his catastrophic mistake and handed Jonah over to the law at last. The thought had given him the only pleasure he'd felt in months.

He hadn't imagined the terrible, lost despair he now saw in Jonah's eyes when he did it.

"Let me say…" Jonah's voice cracked. "Let me tell you. I had to—"

"You didn't. You didn't *have* to. You chose to save yourself and ruin me."

"No. Ben, I know you don't believe me, you never will, but…" He swallowed. "I love you."

Ben stared down. Jonah stared up, eyes wet and glimmering in the gaslight. The white streak in his hair shone.

"How dare you," Ben said at last. The insult was foul beyond belief. A taunting, grotesque parody of what he'd believed, a mockery of his imbecilic passion. "How *dare* you say that. After everything. After you ran away and left me—like that— How stupid do you think I am? You think you just have to whisper something sweet and wiggle your arse and I'll forget what you did to me?"

Jonah shook his head. "I ruined everything, I know, but I swear I couldn't help it—"

Ben's slap cracked across his cheek, sending his head jerking sideways. "Horseshit!"

Jonah put his free hand to his face, a hopeless movement. "I'd change it if I could," he whispered. "I never meant those things to happen to you. I know I hurt you, and you despise me." He gave a little shudder. "I suppose I deserve you to. I'm sorry."

"Stop whining. Damn you to hell, stop it!" Christ, why wasn't he fighting? Ben wanted him to fight. He could beat the man to death, if only he'd fight.

Jonah shook his head. "I love you, Ben."

"I hate you," Ben said, and grabbed for him.

He hadn't intended it. He didn't know what he intended now. His mind was a whirl of rage and misery, and Jonah was lying on the bed as he had so often, with those beseeching blue eyes fixed on Ben, and it had been so long since Ben had cared, or wanted, or felt anything.

He felt now. He wanted Jonah, and he wanted to hurt him.

He lifted Jonah up off the mattress, turning him and throwing him face down, so that he was bent over the bed's edge, kneeling on the floor, his trapped arm twisted awkwardly under him. Jonah grunted and tried to straighten himself, and Ben pushed him down with a palm between the shoulder blades. He fumbled for the fastenings at Jonah's waist, shoved shirttails up, trousers and drawers down to Jonah's knees.

"Ben," Jonah whispered. His voice was thick with tears.

"Shut up." Ben grabbed the bottle of oil. It spilled as he fumbled the top, dripping over his fingers as the gin had dripped from Jonah's. He dragged at buttons, pushed his own clothing aside and knelt behind Jonah's bare arse, smearing the oil over his rigid cock with fingers that shook. Jonah sucked in a sharp breath.

Jesus Christ, what was he doing?

He'd scarcely mustered an erection for someone who'd begged to suck him off. Now he was—was he?—going to force himself on an unwilling man, on Jonah, and he was so hard he felt his own skin could barely contain him.

I'm ruined. I'm broken. What happened to me?

"Shit." He jerked away, sickened, and Jonah twisted round. Ben could see the tears shining in his eyes.

"Jesus, Ben. Please don't—"

"Shut up." Ben's voice was hoarse, unrecognisable to himself. He couldn't do this, of course he couldn't, but to hear the man mewl for mercy would be unbearable. "Shut your mouth."

"Don't stop," Jonah said. "Fuck me. Even if you hate me. Please."

Ben stared at him.

"Please," Jonah repeated. "Once more."

"Turn round." The words didn't sound like his own. "I don't want to see your face."

Jonah turned back. Ben moved forward, like an automaton, thighs wide, covering Jonah. Jonah shifted position, in practised response, knowing just what to do, and if Ben had been hard before, now it was painful. He was aware that he hadn't prepared Jonah, that it would hurt, and part of his mind winced from the knowledge even as another part took a savage pleasure in the fact. A third part, the strongest, knew it didn't matter at all. He was going to fuck Jonah one last time and it would all be over, everything, forever.

"I hate you," he whispered, and thrust in.

Jonah bucked, a little jerk of instinctive distress. Ben repeated, "I hate you," and pushed harder. Jonah was tight around him, breathing hard, not protesting, shifting only in an effort to take him. Ben bore down, past the resisting muscle, feeling himself hold back to make it easier and cursing his weakness at the same moment. He pushed again, until he was fully in Jonah and they both cried out.

"God." Jonah sounded ragged. "Ben."

"You asked for it," Ben rasped, and reached for the bedframe to brace himself.

Then he was fucking. He had never been rough with Jonah before, never wanted to be, and the wrongness of it howled at him as he shoved into Jonah with brutal force, over and over. Jonah whimpered with each thrust, his body moving under Ben's with terrible familiarity. Ben grabbed his piebald hair, jerking his head back. "Don't move. This isn't for you. This is for me."

Jonah whispered acquiescence, body stilling and going limp, and Ben stormed him, keeping his tight grip on Jonah's hair, pounding without regard, grinding his hips against Jonah's body. He fucked Jonah, and muttered words of contempt and hatred in place of the other words he'd used so often, refusing to think about whether Jonah was aroused, what he was thinking. *Do you love me now? Do you?*

It didn't matter. This was vengeance, nothing more. Ben used his calves to trap Jonah's legs to the floor, hissing at every little grunt and gasp he forced from the other man. *I hate you, I hate you...*

God, but he felt good, though. The muscled back that he knew so well, flexing under him, braced against Ben's grip on his hair. Jonah was moving again, pushing back to meet Ben, making incoherent noises that might have been pain, or not, and Ben could only think of burying himself deep in Jonah, making sure the man never forgot him.

"Take it," he gasped in Jonah's ear. "Bloody take it. Say my name."

"Ben." Jonah's head was tilted back as Ben pulled his hair, throat exposed. "Ben. More."

He was aroused, Ben was sure of it. That choke in his voice. Jonah wanted this, and the fact should have disgusted Ben, with Jonah or himself, but dear God, it didn't, and that just made him angrier.

"You bastard." He let go of Jonah's hair and slammed his hips into him, punctuating the words with driving thrusts. "You vicious, worthless swine. I hate you. You know that?"

"I know," Jonah whimpered. "I'm sorry. I'm sorry..."

Ben stared down at Jonah's bowed head, a tangle of black against the linen, its white streak far brighter than the cloth. "I hate you," Ben whispered, and came, with little gasping breaths that might have been sobs.

It was only as the aftershocks subsided through his body that he realised his hand, stretched out to the bedframe, was clutching Jonah's cuffed hand, their fingers tangled together, palm to palm.

He pushed it away. Jonah let his arm fall to the mattress, without protest. Ben jerked out of him, sitting back on his calves, erection wilting fast. Jonah didn't move. He was sprawled half-naked, skin showing the finger marks of brutal use.

He would not ask if Jonah was all right. He would *not*.

The silence stretched out.

"I'm going to take you to the police," Ben said at last. "The Met. You're going to gaol."

"Yes." Jonah's voice was muffled in the sheets. "But I'll run. You do understand that? I always run."

"I won't let you."

"You'll do what you have to." Jonah sounded very weary. "And I'll do the same."

"Of course you will. You already did, and ruined my life with it. Now it's your turn."

Jonah's shoulders sagged into the sheets. "Oh, God, Ben. If you'd just—" He jerked up. "What was that?"

That was a splintering crash from downstairs, and even as Ben's head turned, he heard the unmistakable sound of a police whistle.

"For Christ's sake." Jonah spoke with sudden energy. "It's a raid."

Ben recoiled, as though at a blow. No. Surely not. Not this, not now—

Taken in the act of sodomy in a male meeting house. Another conviction. It would be two years' hard labour this time, a flogging too perhaps, for a shameless recidivist like himself, little more than four months on from his last conviction. He'd been seen all over London's disreputable haunts, the police would know his face. They could convict him on that alone, not to mention the room, and the sheets, and the reek of semen, and the half-naked man chained to the sodding bed.

He couldn't go through it a second time. He could not go back to prison.

"Ben," Jonah said urgently. "Let me go."

His life, what remained of it, was falling to dust, and Jonah could only think of himself. "No. If I'm going down, so are you."

"Ben…" Heavy-shod feet were thundering up stairs and along corridors. There were cries of fear, squeals of protest as doors were flung open. They would come to this room soon. Mechanically, Ben started to tuck himself away, not in the hope of hiding anything, just for a little dignity.

"Ben! Oh, well, sod it." Jonah's free hand delved into his clothing for a second and came out with a twisted wire, and he was rising from the bed, wrist free, before Ben had his buttons fastened.

"What—"

"Give me *some* credit." Jonah pulled his clothing straight. His lip was split and his cheek bruised, but there was just a hint of the old sapphire sparkle dawning in his eyes. "This seems like a good moment to leave." He strode to the window, and Ben realised, with sickening horror, that he was going to do it again. He was going to use that damned witchcraft of his, leave Ben to be arrested, *again*…

"Are you coming?"

"What?"

Jonah threw the window open in a swift movement. "It's about twenty feet to the next rooftop. We can do that. I'll go over first, and you run to me, yes?"

"*What?*" It seemed to be all Ben could say.

"I walk on air, Ben. I can walk you. Just run to me. Or you can stay here and be arrested, but I wish you wouldn't. Let me get us out of here. Please."

"How?"

"Just shut your eyes and run straight over. Pretend you're on the rugby pitch." Jonah's lips gave a tiny twitch. "Score me a try."

There was a crash and a scream from the stairs. The police were on their floor now.

"I'm going." Jonah swung a leg over the sill. "Come after me when I wave. I'll hold you up. Don't stop, don't hesitate. If you stop running, you'll fall." He paused, and gave Ben a tentative smile. "Trust me? Just once more?"

Then he was gone. Ben lunged for the window, sticking his head out, and saw him sprint through the air, a few long strides. He landed with a dancer's turn on the dark tiled roof opposite, twenty feet away and about six feet lower down.

Heavy footsteps approached the door.

If he stayed, it would be two years' hard, and that was a death sentence for many men. If he jumped and fell, it was a death sentence without the trouble of labour, and at least it would all be over. That had been in his mind anyway, once he'd taken his revenge on Jonah, and there was nothing left in his life.

If he could trust Jonah…

He couldn't. It was insane.

He couldn't go back to gaol. Whatever happened, he could not bear that.

Ben swung one leg over the windowsill, then the other. The door of the room slammed open, and a policeman gave a roar, lunging for him. Jonah was perched on the roof opposite, beckoning. Ben shut his eyes and launched himself out into the void.

His foot hit something.

He jerked, and hesitated, and it went from under him, and Jonah screamed, "Run, dammit!" as something else solidified under his flailing foot, pushing him. There was a deep bellow from the window behind him. Ben ran, eyes clamped shut, one stride and another, not thinking. Familiar hands clasped his and pulled, and suddenly he was toppling over and onto Jonah's warm body, and heard his triumphant laugh.

"Did it!" Jonah crowed.

"Oi!" roared a voice from the house opposite. "You there! Oh, how the—"

"Come on," Jonah said urgently. He squirmed up from under Ben, grabbing his hand, and they were running again. It was utter madness. The tiles were steeply pitched, poorly fastened, brittle with age. They cracked under Ben's feet, and he couldn't see a thing, and every step might take them over the edge, plummeting to the stone-flagged street below.

But Jonah's hand was warm on his, holding tight, and when Ben's foot slipped there was a hard, impossible nudge from the air that pushed him back upright.

"Whoa." Jonah pulled them to a halt. They had run along a line of terraced houses, and were at the end of the row. "There." He pointed over, on a diagonal, to where another street joined theirs at a sharp angle. "We're going to windwalk over there, me first, then you, and then we're going to saunter away, all right? Ready?"

"No!" Ben yelped, as Jonah started to disengage his hand. "Jesus!"

Jonah grinned. "Oh, come on. It's fun. Isn't it fun?"

"*Fun?*"

"Fun," Jonah assured him. A police whistle sounded from the street below. "Bugger. Come on, let's be somewhere else. I'll head over there first, I can't do us both at once. Wait for my signal, shut eyes, run. No hesitating. If you stop, you fall. Let's go."

He pulled his hand away, turned, ran. A few lithe steps over nothing and he was on the roof opposite. He held out a hand, grin devilish.

Ben shut his eyes and pushed himself forward, and this time he didn't stop. There was a slight give to whatever was under his feet, a sense of something that would not hold him for long, but the consuming terror that it wouldn't hold him at all was a great deal stronger than any urge to investigate. He crashed onto the roof opposite, and Jonah's arms closed round him, falling backwards against the pitched roofline and onto dry-slimy tiles.

He was over Jonah, with those strong arms around him, and his face buried in Jonah's chest. He smelled of himself, of sweat and spunk, of something Ben thought might be sandalwood, an unfamiliar scent. He was gripping Ben's shoulders, thighs moving apart as if to accommodate the man on top of him, and Ben gasped and opened his eyes.

Jonah was looking up at him, bruised face unreadable in the moon shadows. Ben stared down. There was a long, impossible moment, when neither of them knew what to do, and then Jonah gave Ben a gentle push.

"Up you get. Come on, up. I won't let you fall." Ben made it to his feet, and Jonah gripped his hand once more. He didn't resist. "This row meets another, so it's just a stroll now. On we go."

Ben would not have called it a stroll, slipping and sliding over the roofs of house after house, not looking down, feet cramping with the awkward angle, clambering over attic windows and around chimneys, but at last Jonah stopped. "Up here." He tugged at Ben's hand, and something shoved under his feet. They clambered up, and Ben found himself sitting on a rounded roof ridge, back to a chimneystack, as firmly lodged as it was possible to be on a roof three stories up.

"There." Jonah crouched to sit on the ridge tiles a little further along, and winced as he lowered himself. "Ow."

Shame, staining pitch-dark shame, washed over Ben in waves of heat. "Are you—are you hurt?"

"Well, I'm going to know about it tomorrow," Jonah said. "It's fine."

"I…" Was he sorry? No, he couldn't be. Jonah had deserved it, and worse. He'd betrayed him.

Betrayed him, and saved him.

"I don't understand. I don't understand any of it. How did you—why—"

"Ssh." Jonah shifted closer, tapped Ben on the arm, pointed. "Look."

Ben looked, not sure what he was indicating, and saw London.

The roofscape stretched out in front of him for a mile at least, swards and hills of brick and tile and slate, jaggedly topped by slanting rooflines, pierced by spires and chimneys. The dome of St. Paul's rose molehill-like in the distance. A dark city, huge beyond imagination, made stark and silver by the moon.

"Just look at it a moment," Jonah said softly. "Not many people see this."

They sat, looking out over London in silence. Ben knew he should be shouting, accusing, pushing the bastard off the roof, but that earlier burst of violence had left him feeling hollow and limp, and he was trapped in this suspended moment above the city, not yet ready to break the quiet and the spell.

Nothing had changed, nothing to remedy his pain and anger and hate. Jonah was a thief, a liar, an accessory to murder. But he had said "Score me a try", and the words had stabbed Ben's heart with sweetness.

CHAPTER THREE

Last April

"Oh God, I have to get up," Ben muttered, looking blearily at the daylight through the heavy brown curtains. "It's past nine already."

"Why…oh, rugby." Jonah rolled onto his side, running a hand over the sparse hairs of Ben's chest. He was much hairier, surprisingly so, with a thick wiry tangle of black over his pectoral muscles, his forearms and calves. It gave Ben an odd thrill that he couldn't quite identify. He liked being the bigger man of the two, even though it wasn't by much, he liked the way his solid rugby player's build matched and countered Jonah's athletic strength. But there was something about Jonah's body hair, that incontrovertible evidence of his masculinity, that made Ben feel…not that he was less manly, precisely, but that Jonah was more so. That probably made no sense, he reflected sleepily, and didn't care.

"Rugby," he mumbled, because Jonah's exploring hand was making him think of other games to play. "Get off, Jay. Got to get up."

"Can I come?"

Ben blinked at that. It was not that Jonah was a secret, exactly. Ben had introduced him in the pub, casually, his pal sharing the expenses. It wasn't an unusual arrangement, and to be secretive would attract more attention than openness. Still, to have Jonah come and watch him, in public…

"Not if you don't want." Jonah had read his expression. "I just thought…" There was a little disappointment on his face, perhaps a little hurt, but it was washed away almost at once by the smile. "I just thought I'd like to see you in shorts. Clutching all those big thighs."

"I don't do anything of the sort."

"You play scrum half," Jonah said. "*I* know what that is. All hugging each other and putting your head between their legs. I'm jealous."

"You're a menace," Ben told him, and grabbed his shoulders, rolling him over on top of his own body for a kiss. Jonah came easily at the pull—it was astonishing how light he felt, sometimes, almost weightless—and settled comfortably over Ben, tongue warm and mobile in his mouth, hands exploring.

"Mph," Ben muttered at last. "Got to go."

"I know." Jonah kissed his nose. "I'll wait."

"Come if you like." Ben hadn't meant to say it, but as he did, it seemed absurd not to. For heaven's sake, why shouldn't his pal watch the match? Plenty of locals did, plenty of friends cheered them on. Jonah could cheer him. His secret lover, his Jay, there in the crowd. The thought was a thrill.

"Really?" Jonah's eyes widened. "Can I, Ben?"

He seemed almost childlike in moments like this, as though the tiniest concession was unexpected and thrilling. It squeezed the air from Ben's lungs every time. "Of course you can. I want you watching me."

"Oh, I will." Jonah's smile was brilliant. "Every tackle and scrum and, um…"

"Pass."

"Pass," Jonah agreed. "And score a goal for me."

"Try," Ben said patiently.

"Don't just try, score one." He yelped as Ben rolled him over again, onto his back. "Hey!"

"It's *called* a try, you ape." Ben shook him, laughing. "You'll have to learn the rules."

"I'll learn. And you'll score me a try. And when we come home, I'll do the trying and deal with the tackle."

Ben did score a try—two, in fact, reckless and unbeatable in the knowledge of his lover's eyes on him—and Jonah whooped from the sidelines, a gaggle of new friends already formed around him. Part of the crowd. Part of Ben's life.

"Score me a try," was what Jonah said every game after that, and more often than not, Ben had.

Even at the time, dizzied by the constant ripple of laughter and chatter that had overtaken his quietly ordinary life, and by the bewildering pleasures of Jonah sprawled in his bed, Ben had questions. The most obvious was where the man got his money. Jonah could not read, not even a few words, but his hands showed that he was no manual labourer. *Contract work*, he said when pressed, distracting Ben with a kiss, and every now and then he would disappear for a day or two or three, and come back crackling with gleeful energy and flush with guineas.

Ben didn't ask. He didn't let himself consider if he should. It was perfect, impossibly perfect, and to ask would be to break the enchantment, like the fairytale prince who lit the candle to look on his lover, and lost her. That was a ludicrous thought, himself in that role, but this felt like a fairytale, or a fantasy. Glorious Jonah, with his ever-brimming eyes and his warm, shameless body, and all for staid, straightforward, serious Ben.

There was a night when they lay in each other's arms in the still-hot evening air, a light rain drumming on the open window that neither had the energy to get up and shut. Jonah had fucked him wonderfully, crowing with pleasure as Ben bucked and cried out under him, whispering his name as he came in his turn. Ben held him afterwards, sated and pleasantly sore, and Jonah ducked his head into the crook of Ben's shoulder and said, "I love you."

He said it so freely, so generously, and every time it made Ben's heart stretch a little wider, letting him in.

"I love you too." Ben kissed his tousled black hair. Jonah snuggled down with a satisfied sigh, but Ben couldn't leave it there. "Why?"

"Why what?" Jonah asked. "Why do I love you?"

"Well. Yes."

Jonah gave him a look of some confusion, more amusement. "But why would I not? Of course I love you." He spoke as though it were axiomatic. *I am Jonah, therefore I love Ben.* And the converse would be true, Ben recalled from distant memories of arithmetical logic. *I am Ben, therefore I love Jonah.*

"Because you're perfect. You're extraordinary. I'm so ordinary." Ben didn't feel ordinary in Jonah's arms, and this was pure self-indulgence, but the question still nipped and buzzed around him.

"But you aren't ordinary. You're Benedict Spenser. There's only one of you in the world, and you love me. Nobody's ever been less ordinary than you." Jonah paused, looking at Ben, and the laugh died out of his eyes, leaving deep seriousness. When he next spoke it was more slowly, as if puzzling the words out. "You're not ordinary, Ben, but…you make me feel ordinary."

"You? What do you mean?"

"I don't mean boring. I mean… You make me feel as though there's nothing different about me. That there's no reason anyone should hate me or condemn me or arrest me, or even look at me twice. I'm just an ordinary man quietly getting on with his quiet life, and I'm doing it with you." Jonah smiled up at him. It was a gentler, more serious smile than the usual blinding sparkle, and it thrilled Ben all the more deeply for that. "It's wonderful."

Ben thought he knew what Jonah meant, that he was referring to their illicit affections. He had no idea that it was as close as his lover would come to a confession.

Now

A cat poked its head around a chimneypot and made Ben jump out of his reverie. Jonah laughed, that merry laugh that had been missing from Ben's life so long.

"The cuff," Ben said abruptly. "You could have picked it. Freed yourself."

"I could, yes. More to the point, I'm a practitioner, Ben. I can manipulate the ether, the air around us. Your thoughts. I can do…a lot of things. I could have stopped you putting it on me at all."

"Why didn't you?"

Jonah gave a one-shouldered shrug. He wriggled down the roof so that he could lie back on the tiles, bracing himself with a foot against the gutter.

Ben looked at him, his own hands, the roof tiles, and then out, over the night city. "Why didn't you tell me what you were?" As if that was the most important thing, but it was the answer Ben needed now.

"I didn't want to." Jonah's voice was calm and remote. "I didn't want you to know. I wanted you to see *me*. Not a windwalker or a practitioner. Not a thief. Not what I do, or what I can do, just who I am. Just Jonah, who loved you. If I'd told you—what would I have said? *By the way, lover, I walk on air. By the way, I've been stealing for a living since I was twelve. By the way, you can't trust me.*" He stared up at the sky. "I didn't want that to be true. I wanted to be someone else. With you."

Ben clamped his lips together, squeezed his nails into his palms.

"I'm not very good at planning," Jonah went on. "I should have known I couldn't stay in one place, or if I did, that I had to travel further to steal more safely. I didn't. I wanted to be with you, not go off to steal in Manchester or Birmingham. It was stupid. I do know that, but I…believed it would work, I believed in us and we seemed to be charmed. Until they found me."

"They found you, and you ran," Ben managed. "You used me and you left me behind, and they put me in prison for it."

The night lay between and over them like a quilt.

"Was it bad, in gaol?" Jonah asked at last.

That question was so enraging, so utterly Jonah. "Yes," Ben said distantly. "It was very bad."

"And you lost your job."

"Dismissed with dishonour." The words were sour in his mouth. "They stripped me of my post, while people watched. The landlord evicted us. My parents disowned me."

"Oh God." Jonah had met Ben's parents, dropped by with him for tea. *Nice chap. Our Benedict's pal.* "Oh, Ben."

"They'll never speak to me again." Ben had to swallow hard against that thought. His voice shook. "I lost them, I lost *everything* when I lost you. When you left me behind."

Jonah stared at the moon. "I want to tell you why," he said at last. "Why I ran then."

Ben felt the anger rise. "You already told me." He mimicked Jonah's voice. "You always run."

Jonah sat up, a quick, fluid movement that made Ben flinch with an instinctive fear of the drop that yawned below them. "I don't ask you to like it or to forgive me. I don't expect that. But if you'll listen—"

"No. I don't want to."

"Why not?"

"Because I don't want to know!" Ben shouted. "I don't want to know what was more important than me!"

His voice echoed flatly off the roof tiles. Below them, a dog gave a single gruff yelp.

"I could tell you—" Jonah began.

"It doesn't matter. I don't care. The way you left me there, you sent me to gaol as surely as if you'd testified against me. There's nothing you can say that would change anything."

"It won't change that. But if you understood—"

"I'll never understand. Or, no. I already do. You said you loved me, but you saved yourself. That's all there is."

They stared at each other, lost in hurt, the three feet between them a chasm.

"Will you meet me?" Jonah asked at last.

"What? Why?"

"Let's say Regent's Park. Queen Mary's Gardens, tomorrow at four. If you were ready to listen to me, I could tell you things, and if you're not, we'll…talk about something else, I suppose."

"Is there anything else to talk about?"

"I don't know." Jonah pulled his knees to his chest, hunching over himself. "Maybe not. We could find out, if you come." He glanced at Ben, hesitant and silenced, and went on, "Well, I'll be there. And if you're not there, I'll be there next Wednesday at four, and the next, and the next, until I have to leave London, which may happen. But I'll keep coming back, when I can. In case you want to hear."

Ben rubbed his hands over his eyes. He felt drained. "Jonah…"

"I can't do much else," Jonah said. "I made all the wrong decisions. I'm not very good at planning. I made a terrible mess of you, of us, but I can give you some sort of explanation, when you want to hear it. Or if you want to hate me forever and never know why, you can do that too. I don't have many choices left."

"And what if I turn up tomorrow with the Met and the justiciary for you?"

"Then I'll run."

"Naturally you will." Ben rested his head against the brickwork. The night chill was coming on, biting through his thin coat. "All right. You'll be at Queen Mary's Gardens, at four. I…I'll think about it."

Jonah nodded. "I'll get you down now, if you like. The police will be long gone." He reached out a hand, standing steady on the roof, and Ben took it, rising far more cautiously. Jonah was washed clean by moonlight, the blood and bruising Ben had inflicted mere shadows under his piebald hair, and Ben wanted for a stupid, painful instant to kiss the lines of his throat and the generous curve of his mouth, to see him smile again.

Of course Jonah was not callous or uncaring. He never had been. Ben had made him into a monster in his mind, because it had kept him sane to do so, but this was the reality: a deeply flawed man, a thief, a coward who ran away. He had saved Ben this evening because he could, but he had left him when he could not, and Ben knew, with a sullen weight on his heart, that the explanation Jonah promised would be no more than that bare, sad truth of self-preservation at all costs, dressed in fine words. A jackdaw in peacock's feathers.

Perhaps Ben could stop hating him, though. That would be something, a small victory against the loneliness, if he could not be full of hate.

"Nobody about." Jonah was peering over the rooftop. "Come on, I'll take you back to earth."

Ben barely slept that night. He probably wouldn't have slept anyway, but it didn't help that, every time he closed his eyes, he saw the first lurching step into empty air. The fact that he'd had his eyes shut was neither here nor there: his imagination painted a yawning chasm into which he tumbled, as Jonah laughed from the house opposite.

He couldn't sleep, and he couldn't decide what to do.

He could go to the justiciary. Bring them along to Regent's Park. Perhaps Jonah would escape, but at least he would have done his duty.

He could walk away. Leave London, go home—no, there was no home. Go *somewhere*. Take a new name, start a new life, leave all this behind. Forget about vengeance, forget about betrayal, remember only never to trust or to leave himself open to another person ever again. That wasn't Ben's way, but perhaps that had been his mistake.

Or he could step over the parapet of the nearest bridge, over the turbid waters of the Thames, and jump. That had tugged at him for long months, the urge for this to be over because there was nothing to carry on for.

(Jonah, under him, grinding back against his thrusts. Jonah holding out his hand as Ben ran impossibly towards him.)

Ben lay awake for hours, thinking of all the options, all the different paths to an empty future. When he slept at last, it was to be awakened far too soon by the stir around him, as the other men in the cheap, stinking dosshouse rose off their pallets, preparing for another day of survival. He washed under the cold pump water, ignoring the ridicule of a pair of urchins, who felt that cleanliness came a very poor second to warmth. As he shivered and dried himself with his grubby towel, he could see their point.

He went to look for employment that day, joining the loose crowds of men who offered themselves for manual labour. He was becoming too shabby for anything except labouring work, but London was full of jobless men, scrabbling for piecework, anything to keep the wolf away, and he was one among hungry thousands.

There was nothing. He put his name down with a few hard-eyed men who claimed they could find him work, for a share of the few pence it might bring in, and lunched on a hot, greasy slab of suet pudding that filled his stomach, much as concrete might. At four o'clock he was sitting on a bench in Queen Mary's Gardens, looking at the blossom and the crocuses bursting through bare, dry earth.

"Ben." There was hesitancy in Jonah's voice, from behind the bench, and pleasure, and Ben had to take a deep breath to stay still and controlled.

"I'm here. What do you want to talk about?"

"Shall we walk?"

Ben stood, turning, and Jonah's black brows snapped together. "Are you all right? You look—"

"Tired. I'm tired."

Tired, and hungry, and shabby, and Jonah in clean linens with a smart blue waistcoat setting off his eyes, even though his face was still marked by Ben's blows. Resentment surged. Ben turned on his heel and set off, not waiting. Jonah caught up after a couple of strides. He didn't speak, simply pacing Ben.

Ben wanted to ask, didn't want to. He said, instead, "Tell me about the murders."

"Murders?"

"Dead policemen. You must remember."

"Well, yes, but that wasn't *me*." Jonah sounded mildly indignant.

"It was your gang. That's what the justiciars said. Your criminal associates—"

"Hold your horses. I don't know what they told you, but I've never had a gang."

"They said there were four of you."

"There were *three*, of *them*, and me," Jonah said with precision. "I don't join things, Ben. I don't join gangs, or the justiciary, or trade unions, or the Quakers, or anyone else. Look, there was a warlock. A harpy of a woman named Lady Bruton, and she had a painter working for her. God, the painter. I hated that man. I'd have killed him if I could."

"A painter?" Ben asked blankly. "Why?"

Jonah shuddered. "He was a murderer. He painted people and killed them by destroying the picture. He didn't care who, or why, he just liked doing it. *Really* liked it, Ben, it made him hard. Lady Bruton gave him a series of victims, and he did whatever he was told."

"As you did?"

Jonah's lower lip jutted, mulish. "Lady Bruton had me by the short hairs. She needed a windwalker to carry out a chunk of her plan, and she found me. I didn't *want* to work for her. She made me do it."

"Oh, come on. Do you have any idea how often I hear that?"

Jonah swung round, face dark. "I'm not making excuses. Lady Bruton was hellish strong and I never even had proper training. She could have taken me apart on her own. For pity's sake, she and the painter got Stephen Day on his knees—one of the senior justiciars, an absolute sod—and I shouldn't like to meet someone more powerful than him in a dark alley. Or more tiresomely self-righteous," he added, with feeling. "Ghastly little man, but strong as hell. If Bruton could get *him* down, I didn't stand a chance."

"What about the policemen? Who killed them?"

"The painter. Lady Bruton's orders."

"And you let them die?"

Jonah made a frustrated noise. "What was I supposed to do, run to the justiciary? You don't understand, Ben. I was completely on my own—"

"Whose fault was that?" Ben snarled. "You were looking out for number one, even if it meant abandoning me and killing people."

"I *didn't*—"

"You might as well have done. If you stand by and watch while your employer commits murder and you don't do a damn thing to stop it, that makes you guilty. In law, in common decency, in everything."

"Oh, so I should have just sacrificed myself on the altar of virtue, should I?" Jonah said with heat. "Let Bruton destroy me for the sake of people I never even met? What the devil would a pack of coppers have done for me, except send me to prison with hard labour?"

"God, Jonah. You don't decide whether you're going to let someone die on the basis of how much use they are to you."

"I look out for myself. Because nobody else does. And I'm sorry if you think I should have cared more about people I don't know than people I do, but if you just let me tell you—"

"I don't want to hear it." Ben turned on his heel, hurrying away.

"Ben!" Jonah sprinted after him. "Will you let me *talk*?"

Ben stopped and swung to face him, almost colliding. Jonah was a few inches shorter, just enough that he had to turn his face up and Ben to dip his head for a kiss. He glared down now as though they had never touched, never met except in anger.

"I don't want to talk," he gritted out. "I don't want to hear this. You're—" He glanced around swiftly but they were alone on the path. "You're not the man I fell in love with. That was a lie, all along, *your* lie, because I'd never have loved such a self-centred callous swine as you. Go away."

Jonah stood, speechless, expression raw, as Ben turned, striding down the path, he didn't know where to. He cursed himself. He shouldn't have gone, should have known it would be nothing but lies and excuses, but Jonah was like an open sore that he kept prodding, making the infection worse.

"Ben," Jonah called from behind him. "I'll come back. Here tomorrow, same time. I'll wait for you."

"You can wait forever," Ben said aloud, to himself or the air, and strode on.

CHAPTER FOUR

Last autumn

They lasted a handful of blissful months, March to October, with long walks through the summer woods and fields, endless lovemaking, sometimes a drink in the pub where Spenser's pal Pastern was now a casually accepted face—though never when drinking with his police colleagues—and Ben's favourite thing of all, nights together downstairs in the little cottage, Ben in the big winged chair and Jonah on the floor, leaning against his legs, while Ben read to him. They read *Bleak House* and *Dombey and Son* and *The Old Curiosity Shop*, which made Jonah cry, and laugh at himself through his tears. It was the most joyous time of Ben's life.

Then Jonah burned it all down.

The end was already coming in September, though Ben didn't know it. That was when daring cat burglaries of offices and grand houses in Hertfordshire had reached such a number that the outraged wealthy of the county had begun putting pressure on the chief superintendent to get results. That was when the justiciars came.

Ben hadn't dealt with justiciars before. He knew *of* them: the funny ones, the not-quite-police who dealt with peculiar cases. Not uniformed, not disciplined, all of them with an odd air of confidence and a habit of unhelpful remarks and abrupt disappearance. These two were Miss Nodder, a freckled, authoritative, green-eyed woman, and a dark unkempt man named Webster who smoked Turkish cigars with unnerving intensity. They had been all round Hertfordshire, he heard, with access to the files on the burglaries, and now they settled in Berkhamsted, appearing and disappearing, claiming an office in the police station and evicting its previous occupant without consultation. The scuttlebutt was that they were closing in on the cat burglar here.

A couple of weeks after the justiciars arrived, one bright October day, they called in four men, Ben among them, and announced they had been requisitioned for a special job. The cat burglar was known to be setting his sights on the Tring Museum. The justiciars would wait there, take the man in the act, the following night. The constables would act as backup, extra manpower, in case it was needed. They had been chosen, Miss Nodder told them, for their steadiness and discretion. They were men who would not panic or speak loosely. They would be trustworthy, she said with certainty, and her voice carried a very slight note of "or else".

Ben would have told Jonah all about it. He told Jonah everything, always, glorying in his passionate interest and the glow of happy pride any of Ben's small successes brought to his eyes. He had told him about the investigation into the robberies, prompted by Jonah's endless curiosity, and he would not have thought twice about breaking Miss Nodder's injunction that none of them should speak of this at all. It was Jonah, for heaven's sake. Ben could trust him.

He didn't have the chance. Jonah didn't come home until very late that night, and slipped into bed sometime in the small hours. He didn't talk, simply held Ben close, fiercely, almost desperately. The next morning he was gone before Ben arose.

So Ben waited in the Tring Museum that night, in the silent dark, with the shadowy forms of long-dead things all around him.

He was in the main hall, on the ground floor, near the great wooden door, a fellow constable on the other side of the room. The first floor was mostly open, just a walkway round the walls lined with cases, so he could see up to the ceiling.

He was expecting something—the justiciars had seemed quite certain of that—but it was still a jolting shock as angry voices shattered the silence. There was a crash from the first floor, and a flare of some bright yellow light, and Ben saw a dark shape run to the railings that ringed the first-floor landing, and vault the iron with effortless grace, leaping over to the thirty-foot drop onto marble below.

He cried out, thinking he had seen a man plunge to his death, and then he cried again because the man didn't fall. He landed on thin air as though it was solid ground, foot braced on nothing, ran a few steps, and hurled himself sideways as something like a rush of wind hissed through the air, making Ben's ears pop.

The other copper was swearing devoutly, gaping up. Miss Nodder leaned over the balcony, making another throwing gesture, green eyes narrow and intent and glowing like a cat's. The burglar was changing direction in midair, leaping like a squirrel bouncing between branches, and Ben heard him laugh aloud.

That laugh.

It couldn't be.

Ben stared up, mouth open in sickened shock, as the burglar danced through the air above him. The burglar looked down, and their eyes met.

Jonah's gleeful, wild smile dropped away. He dropped too, suddenly scrabbling at the air, as if whatever held him up had vanished. He lunged out for an invisible handhold, pulling himself up as something sizzled through the room above his head. Jonah glanced round, and at Ben one last time, and then he was moving once more, diving through a window on the ground floor that broke before he was anywhere near it.

He was gone, leaving Miss Nodder shouting orders from the balcony, and Ben with a gaping hole in his chest that he knew nothing would ever fill again.

Now

Ben had given the justiciary a public house as his address for contact, since he had not wanted to admit he was sleeping in a dosshouse, and he had not been sure if he wanted them to find him. It was the Red Lion, just down the road from his grimy lodgings, where gangmasters gathered to look for casual work, and when he went in there the next morning he was greeted by the landlord's cry.

"Hoi, mate! Constable Marshall, right?"

Reddening, aware of the scornful glances cast at his shabby clothing, Ben took the letter the man held out. It was a tersely worded request for his attendance at eleven that morning from Peter Janossi, giving no detail of the reason.

He couldn't imagine why the justiciary wanted him. He didn't need them now, and he should be looking for work. But the fruitless search was draining, and this might be useful, and he was curious. He breakfasted on a stale roll and coffee from a street stall, and killed the time till the meeting in a church, for the sake of the seat and the quiet.

At eleven he was at the Council, being shown in to Janossi's office. The justiciar had been joined by another man, a small, rather shabbily dressed fellow with a mop of dark red curls that needed cutting. He looked rather younger than Ben's own twenty-six years, except for the lines round his remarkably vivid golden eyes. He stood, holding out a hand, and Ben was startled to see that he was no more than five feet tall.

"Stephen Day," said the short man, and his fingers closed around Ben's.

"God!" Ben recoiled at the electric crackle against his skin, snatching away his hand. It felt as though it had been bitten by a snake.

"Sorry," said Day. "My hands do that. Are you Constable Marshall, of Hertfordshire?"

"Yes, sir." Ben held himself straight. It seemed prudent. Day didn't look like much, but he remembered Jonah's words. *Senior justiciar. Absolute sod.*

"And you're looking to arrest Jonah Pastern."

"Sir."

"Sit down." Day waved him to a chair. "I'm very happy you're here, Constable Marshall. Have you found any indication that Pastern's still in London?"

Ben had thought about how he would answer that, sitting in the church. He had resolved that he would tell the truth. Jonah could not expect his protection, and what he expected didn't matter anyway. He stood convicted out of his own mouth, and Ben could not mislead officers of the law.

That was what he'd decided. Now he said, "I've some useful leads, sir."

"Oh, good. Well, we may be able to help you." Day pulled over a manila folder that sat on the desk. "Has anyone told you about the painter?"

Ben couldn't remember if Janossi had told him or not. He went for safety. "If you could, sir."

"One of Pastern's criminal associates. He drew people, and destroyed the pictures, and that killed them. He killed a man in front of my eyes." Day's voice was calm and level, but Ben found himself sitting straight, skin prickling. "He drew a friend of mine, and threatened to tear the picture up to force my obedience. Pastern was working under the same threat."

He said that in an informative sort of way, as if it was just a simple fact, hardly important at all. "The threat of a picture?" Ben repeated. "A picture of whom?"

"Precisely," said Day, seeming not to hear the last question. "Newhouse drew a picture and held that threat over Pastern's head. I don't think much of Jonah Pastern. A dangerous, amoral, self-centred piece of work." There was quite a lot of feeling in Day's voice. "But there is no doubt that he did Lady Bruton's bidding because of the picture. When its threat was lifted he was off like a rat up a drainpipe."

Ben nodded, numb.

"I'm sure you're wondering how we know this," Day went on. "In his hurry to save his skin, once he was sure the picture had been rendered harmless, Pastern left it behind. We picked it up and filed it, and Joss here, in a praiseworthy effort to help your search, actually found the file, which is impressive even for his powers of vision. Hence, we called you here. We thought it might be useful if you had a picture of the one person Pastern cares about who isn't Jonah Pastern. You might be able to track the fellow down. Ask some questions about who he is and what he knows. That's what I'd do."

Ben's mouth was sandpaper-dry and there was blackness at the edges of his vision. A man Jonah cared about. Could that be the excuse, the explanation for what Ben had been through? Another man?

No. Anything but that.

"Would you like to see it? It may be enlightening."

Ben couldn't speak. He managed a jerk of the head.

The justiciar opened a file, flicked out a sheet of thick artist's paper. It was stained brown with what looked like dried blood, and torn in several places, with straight careful deliberate rips from the edge. Day turned it over to show the sketch, and put it on the desk.

Ben looked down at his own face.

There was a second's total silence, then he sprang from his chair—

Except he didn't, because though he felt the surge of his muscles, something had clamped round him, holding arms and legs as though they were glued down, giving his limbs the leaden feel of a nightmare. He strained uselessly, with a rising sense of terrified helplessness, but his efforts made no difference at all.

"No, you stay there, Constable Marshall." Day walked round the desk. "Well, I say Marshall. Joss was quite startled when he found this picture, so we sent someone down to Hertfordshire with it. *Is this Constable Marshall*, she asked them. In fact, she asked Constable Marshall himself, it turned out. That didn't go down well. I don't think he was very happy to learn you were using his name." He hopped up to perch on the edge of the desk. "You're Benedict Spenser. There's a name to conjure with, having read Pastern's file."

Ben pushed back against the invisible bonds, to no effect. He couldn't move and, he realised, he couldn't speak. He was trapped like a fly on flypaper. His heart was pounding with a hollow thump, lungs tight with fear.

Day went on, thoughtfully. "Benedict Spenser. Constable Spenser, before your dismissal from the force. The man who was living with Jonah Pastern."

"As man and wife," Janossi put in derisively.

"I'm speaking, Joss." Day's voice was quite calm, but Janossi's mouth clamped shut. "The man who helped Pastern escape arrest. The man Pastern left behind to suffer in his place. How was that for you?" He smiled. It didn't touch his eyes. "Jonah Pastern's lover, abandoned to his own cost, then preserved at the cost of four other lives. Lives of actual policemen, Mr. Spenser, not corrupt, dishonourably discharged ones who associate with felons. And here you are now, wasting our time, making a mock of us. I don't like any of those things." He leaned forward. "I'm not inclined to like you."

It was quite mutual. Ben stared at the glowing gold eyes of the frightening little man opposite him. He couldn't move, and he could barely think for all he'd been told.

Jonah. Him. His picture.

Dear God, had he truly meant it? If Jonah had loved him, if he had done all these terrible things to protect him…

If Jonah had let four men die for him. Oh, sweet Jesus, no.

Day was looking at him, expression quizzical. "It's an odd thing, you turning up here. We couldn't decide if you were trying to pick up your partner in crime after you'd got out, or if you were the spurned lover coming for revenge. That became more obvious after the other night. You may not know this, and Pastern certainly doesn't, but we expect practitioners to behave with a certain discretion in public. A little restraint. *Not* windwalking out of a whorehouse window. Really, ex-Constable? The joys of reunion, and you have to make a spectacle of yourselves and rub the Met's noses in Jonah blasted Pastern's existence, *again*?"

"Typical mary-anns," Janossi said, coming in hard and scornful. "No self-control."

Day paused, just a fraction of a second. "Am I keeping you from your work, Joss?"

"No, sir."

"I'm sure you must have some paperwork to do."

"Well, yes, but this is my office," Janossi pointed out with a grin. "It's all in here."

"So go and do something that isn't paperwork, somewhere else." Day's tone remained pleasant, but Janossi opened his mouth, shut it, and left without a word.

Day looked after him until the door shut, and turned back to Ben. "What exactly do you think I'm going to do now, Mr. Spenser?"

Ben stared back at him, unable to respond. Day raised a brow, then said, "Oh, yes, I beg your pardon," and quite suddenly the force that clamped Ben's jaw and throat was no longer there.

He took a gasping breath and a moment to steady himself before replying, "I have no idea."

"You're well out of your depth, aren't you? I don't suppose your last time in gaol was very pleasant, and believe me, it will be a great deal worse in London. Bad enough if it's for gross indecency, but if you're also there for aiding and abetting a murderer—"

"I knew nothing of the murders before you told me," Ben said urgently. "Nothing."

Day sighed. "I'm inclined to believe you, as it happens. But the Met may not. They need a scapegoat of some kind, and everyone else is dead. And you did let him go."

"He got away," Ben insisted. "He tricked me."

Day made a face. "He used you, fooled you, left you to face the music, you did the hard time, and now you're chasing after him. Why is that?"

"I…" Ben didn't know, couldn't say any more. That brief, vengeful fuck, and the rooftop escape, and the picture that stared up at him from the desk…

"He's not an evil man, unfortunately," Day observed.

"Unfortunately?"

"Oh, yes. That makes him all the more harmful. If he was evil, we'd kill him. No, he's…chaotic. He's left a lot of trouble in his wake. It has to stop, Mr. Spenser. You were a policeman, till he ruined you: you must know it has to stop. If he would just go away, or be discreet…but he won't, and isn't, and it seems he can't be. And he will go on causing havoc until he's prevented. Look at you. What has he done to you?" Day's voice was sympathetic, almost unbearably so. "The worst thing is, I'd believe his intentions were good."

He tapped the sketch, where one of the long tears reached almost to the pencilled face. "I saw the painter at work. I know how it was. He'll have torn the paper, slowly, till the rip reached almost to your skull, and if it had reached there your troubles would have been over. Pastern didn't let that happen. But at what cost, to you, to the dead men, very nearly to me and those close to me? At what cost to everyone, now that the Metropolitan Police and London's practitioners are at loggerheads? How much trouble can he be allowed to cause?"

"I know, sir. I know."

"God knows I sympathise, Spenser," Day said softly. "Sometimes the wrong person is…inches away from being the right one. And vice versa." A fleeting, foxlike smile twitched at his lips. "But you need to give him up. He's an airborne catastrophe. Help us get him off the streets. I may even be able to help you in return."

"I don't know where he is."

"Yes, you do," Day said. "He's in London. He's told you some things—you clearly knew about the painter—but not all, because you didn't know about the picture of you. You've an expressive face," he added, at Ben's look. "You're talking to him. He cares about you. Therefore, you have an assignation, or a place to look, or some way of meeting him. Don't you?"

Ben concentrated on keeping his features still. He knew damned well that he didn't have an expressive face. Day had disturbingly clear sight.

"I can help you," Day repeated. "I can't wipe your record but I can put in a good word. Get you off the hook with the Met. You can take a new name, live without looking over your shoulder. Make a new start. What are you doing now, looking for piecework? Hauling bricks? Are you even eating properly?" He cocked his head to one side with a slight frown. "Don't be a fool, Spenser. Tell us where to find Pastern. We'll pick him up and pin him down, and your life can start again."

"Pin him down," Ben said. "You mean, cripple him?"

Day's russet brows drew together. "Who said that?"

"Mrs. Gold."

"Of course she did," Day muttered. "Frankly, then…if he can't control his powers, they'll have to be controlled for him. He can't just dance through the sky taunting the Metropolitan Police. I'm not going to lie to you. We will probably hobble him, yes."

Ben swallowed. "I can't…"

"Can't do that to him? Can't ask him to face the direct consequences of his own actions, so that instead you have to pay, for the rest of your life, serving another gaol sentence for something we both know you didn't intend, slipping further into poverty and degradation, while he goes blithely on his way? Is he worth that?"

"No. I know."

"If he was worth it, he'd hand himself in rather than watch you suffer. Do you think he will?"

"He saved me from the painter," Ben said, clinging to that.

"He bartered four lives for yours. But the point is, Spenser, those were *other people*. Not himself. It's his skin at stake now. Perhaps you know him better than I do, but…"

Ben stared ahead, unseeing, adrift. He didn't know what he owed Jonah, or if he could forget what had happened. He knew what he should do, in the interests of justice, no matter Jonah's motives. He was still so much a policeman, even if they'd taken that from him.

But to cripple him, to bring that glittering spirit to the ground…

"You can talk to me, in confidence," Day said gently. "You might as well. It's not going to get any worse for you. And I do understand."

"Do you?"

"More than anyone else will, certainly. Here." The bonds that held Ben down shivered away. He jerked his arms up from the chair, in involuntary reaction. He didn't try to escape. That, it was quite clear, would not happen.

"Now." Day tipped his head to the side. "You loved him?"

"Yes," Ben said, defying Day, and the world, and his own damned stupidity. "Yes, I loved him."

"And now?"

"He left me. He put me in gaol. He ruined me. What do you think?"

Day shrugged. "Tell me."

Ben met his eyes for a few angry, bewildered seconds, and leaned forward, putting his head in his hands. "I don't know," he said, voice muffled. "I don't know what's right any more."

"I'm sure you don't. You poor swine." The sympathy in Day's voice was worse than hate. "Really, is there not another man in all England you could have loved?"

"I don't think so. There was never anyone else. And he made me laugh."

Day was silent for a moment. At last he said, "Look, Spenser, you have to give him up. You know that. I can make you do it." Ben looked up at that, sharply. Day reached out a hand, but didn't touch him. "I can fluence you—influence your mind, your thoughts. You'll tell me anything I want, and there is nothing you can do to stop me. It would not be your choice."

It wasn't a threat. It was far, far worse than a threat. It was a kindness.

"No," Ben said.

"I need Pastern, one way or the other. Justice requires it. Or, at least, the justiciary do."

"Yes." Ben took a deep breath. "Queen Mary's Gardens, in Regent's Park. He'll be there at four."

Day nodded. "Thank you. You've done the right thing." He hopped off the table. "We'll keep you here till then. I'll organise some food. Try not to think about it now. Things will get better from here, believe me."

CHAPTER FIVE

Ben spent the next few hours in a small bare room. It wasn't exactly a cell. The door was definitely closed on him, but there was a comfortable chair, books and periodicals, and he was brought a jug of ale and a huge plateful of steaming steak and kidney pudding. He devoured it, the richness of the greasy meat making him almost giddy. It should have been ashes in his mouth, after his betrayal, but in fact it was the best meal he'd had in months.

He'd given Jonah up. They would arrest him, hobble him, gaol him, and Ben would walk away a free man, with his revenge. He'd be a damned fool to do otherwise. Jonah hadn't hesitated to save his skin at Ben's expense, to twist and lie and manipulate him.

The picture, and that wild rooftop escape, throbbed in his mind. Jonah hadn't abandoned him altogether. Jonah still cared for him, somehow.

But their charmed existence had been a fantasy, based on lies. Jonah had said it was just them, just two ordinary men loving each other, but that hadn't been true. They had been a copper and a thief, a liar and a dupe, and their idyllic few months had only been possible because of Jonah's deceit and Ben's wilful blindness.

Now one of them had to pay for what happened. One of them had to go to gaol. And there was no doubt at all that it was Jonah's turn.

Last October

Nobody blamed Ben for his failure to apprehend the burglar.

"You couldn't be expected to cope with that," Miss Nodder told them the next morning. She was talking to Ben, Constable Marshall, and the other two policemen who'd witnessed Jonah's flight. "You weren't expecting it. Our responsibility. We try not to tell people too much of what they might encounter in case they panic, and then if they do encounter it, they're shocked. It can't be helped. You'll know next time."

"What is he?" Ben managed to ask. His voice didn't sound at all out of the ordinary, he thought, considering his exhaustion. He had sat up at home the whole night, waiting. Jonah hadn't come back. "How did he do that?"

"He's what we call a windwalker," Miss Nodder said. "He can make the air bear him. That means he's a blasted nuisance to get hold of. And he has other skills too." She looked from Ben to the other men. "I believe I need to tell you about practitioners."

Jonah didn't come back to the cottage that night either. Ben sat up again, in the winged chair where he had so often read to Jonah, *Our Mutual Friend* abandoned on the table. He meant to wait all night, though he didn't expect a visit, and if he received one, he didn't know what he would do.

Jonah, his Jonah, was a magician. That was what "practitioner" meant, someone with unnatural powers. The ability to walk on air, or exert force on objects, or change a man's thoughts.

Had he changed Ben's thoughts? Ben had loved him so hard, so fast, falling into his arms and his life as though Jonah had been the missing piece of his existence. Had Jonah made him believe that? Was it all a lie? Nothing else about him had been true.

He had certainly pumped Ben for information. All those artless questions about work, about the robberies, and the investigation…

If he'd come back in time that night before the burglary, Ben would have told him about the trap laid at the Tring Museum, and Jonah wouldn't have gone, and Ben might never have known that his lover was a traitor, and a magician, and a thief. He would have had lying, duplicitous Jonah in his bed now, and never known the truth.

He wished, more than anything in the world, that Jonah was here and he didn't know.

The disaster that was overtaking him was too great for Ben to understand. Realisations burst in his mind like gunfire: the cottage that he could not afford alone, the appalling inevitability of the discovery that he had been living with Jonah, the likelihood that their true relationship would be discovered. The thoughts came on him sickeningly and died away, to be replaced by others just as bad, and at the centre of it all was the great airless darkness inside him where Jonah's bright smile had been.

Ben stared at the ashes in their hearth, long after the candle guttered and died, until dawn greyed the windows, and then he got up and went to work because he couldn't think what else to do.

Halfway through the morning, a messenger sent by Miss Nodder burst in.

"Men. Now. We've found Pastern."

Ben and Marshall were among the last on the scene. It seemed Jonah had been hiding in the timber yard down by the canal, and it seemed as though he had resisted arrest. The justiciar Webster was nursing a bloody nose, there were hysterical sobs from somewhere in the milling crowd of bewildered people, and the great carved totem pole all the way from America that adorned the timber yard lolled drunkenly to one side. Jonah was face down on the ground, swearing and spitting, with three constables sitting on him. His wrists were handcuffed behind his back, and a fourth man was awkwardly cuffing his ankles together.

As Ben stared at the filthy, struggling criminal, his lover, he heard an ominous rumble from the timber yard, and a crash that shook the ground.

"That's the bloody logpile going again!" Webster leapt up. "All men, get in there, follow Miss Nodder's orders. Someone, get that flying bastard in the carriage and *keep* him in there."

"I will," Ben said.

He dragged Jonah up and hauled him, filthy and wild, to the police cab. The horse neighed nervously as he approached. He half pushed Jonah in, since his ankles were so tightly tethered he couldn't go up the step, and then he shut the door and sat on the hard bench, opposite the man who had ruined him.

"Ben." Jonah had a split lip, and his tongue dipped at the blood. "Oh God, lover. I'm sorry."

"You're sorry," Ben repeated. "You're *sorry*."

"I am. I didn't mean… Ben, you have to let me go."

"What?" Ben stared at him, incredulous.

Jonah's absurdly blue gaze was melting him with its intensity. "You have to. I can't go to gaol now."

"Perhaps you should have thought of that before you became a bloody thief!"

"I know. I know, I'm sorry, but—" He hesitated, before rushing on. "They'll hobble me, Ben. They'll cut my tendons so I can't windwalk. They'll cripple me and take away my flight and put me in a tiny cell and I'll go mad, I will."

"I'll get a lawyer." Ben cursed himself for his weakness as he spoke. "Someone. Somehow. They'll argue your case—"

"Lawyer," Jonah said with scorn. "I won't even get a trial. I'll just disappear, and they'll hobble me and…I can't be locked up. Please, Ben. Don't let them do that to me. Don't let them take me."

"Christ," Ben said thickly. "Stop."

"I'm so sorry and I shouldn't ask this but I have to. Please just undo the cuffs. Give me a chance."

"You had a chance. *We* had a chance and you—you just—Jesus, Jonah. I *loved* you."

"Don't." Jonah sounded as defeated as he looked. "Don't say that. Don't stop loving me."

"You've ruined me," Ben rasped. "You lied, and you cheated, and you made a fool of me and if I let you go— Go to the devil. I won't be your dupe any longer."

"I didn't lie about us," Jonah said. "I promise. I love you."

Ben clenched his fists. "I don't care!"

"I do." Jonah moved forward, and his lips were on Ben's, warm and bloody and gritty with sawdust. Ben tried to push him away, got a grip on his shoulders to do just that, and Jonah whispered, "Ben, listen to me, love me," and somehow Ben's hands wouldn't let go. Then he was kissing Jonah back, as desperately as that first time when they'd stumbled out of the pub and into the alley, sloppy and wild. Jonah leaned heavily against him, unbalanced by his restraints. He twisted around, and half fell sideways, and Ben went with him, and over him, sprawling on the hard benches of the police carriage. He kissed Jonah with a reckless madness, feeling the lust springing through him as they rolled together on the cramped space of the floor, legs bent and limbs tangled. Jonah squirmed round and hauled him upwards, onto the bench, hands cupping his face, warm and close on Ben's skin. He stared into his eyes, his own cobalt gaze bright with tears.

"I'm so sorry, Ben."

And, as the carriage door opened, just as Ben realised that Jonah's hands were no longer cuffed, his lover leapt out and backwards and up through the air, darting to freedom.

He left behind the police-issue cuffs on his wrists and ankles, both sets opened with the key he'd taken from Ben's pocket as they'd embraced, and he left Ben, mouth red with kisses, clothes dishevelled, face tearstained, helplessly taken in the act.

After that, there was nothing but shame.

He was arrested, inevitably, and interrogated, and it took no time for his living arrangements to be revealed, or for them to become widely known through the station. They kept him in the cells for days, catcalled and spat at by the other prisoners and officers alike. Twice, in the night, the door opened and his fellows came in, shadowy figures as if he wouldn't recognise them. The first beating left him bruised and bloody; the second time he fought back savagely until Marshall kicked him hard enough to crack a rib.

He was absolved of having deliberately freed Jonah. Whether the police believed his protestations that he had not handed over the key, or whether nobody wanted the additional scandal, he didn't know. The justiciars, while cursing him up hill and down dale, admitted that Jonah was known to be extraordinarily talented at picking both pockets and locks, and had escaped on plenty of occasions before this. That accusation was dropped, leaving the gross indecency charge, based on his discovery in the carriage. Ben pleaded guilty to that. He lacked the strength to fight any more, and he could not afford a lawyer, and it was true, all true.

Ben served ten weeks with hard labour for Jonah's last Judas kiss. He did the kind of time that could be expected for a bent copper and a mary-ann. The other prisoners despised him, and showed it; the guards would not protect him. Sometimes they watched and laughed, or made bets. Ben fought when he could, at first out of terror of what might be done to him if he didn't resist, later because hitting out at other men, without restraint or rules, brought him some kind of satisfaction. It came to a head when a red-faced fellow, maddened by forced abstinence from gin, went for Ben with a broken bottle. He broke the man's jaw, though not before the jagged glass ripped his temple. At least the relentlessness of the harassment dropped off afterwards.

On his release, he was dishonourably discharged from the police force, to the open contempt of men who had been friends. And when he returned, aching and soul-weary, to his parents' home, they did not open the door. His father hissed his rejection and disgust from a part-opened window, while in the room behind, his mother wept.

He had no career, no reputation, no friends, no family. All of it gone. Jonah had burned through his life and left it waste to save himself.

Now

Some few minutes after the distant chime of three o'clock, Day and Janossi came for him in the cell, along with a young woman. She was slender, sharp-featured, with a measuring look in her silver-blue eyes, and she was wearing boy's clothes: trousers, a sack jacket and a cap, with long blonde hair falling from beneath it.

"This is Miss Saint, our windwalker," Day said. "She has a few questions to ask you."

"Yeah, I do." Saint planted her hands on her slim hips. "The peelers said you windwalked, with Pastern. They saw you. But you ain't a windwalker. So what was that? How'd that work?"

"I don't know. Jonah did it. He said he'd walk me."

"What did he say to do?" Saint demanded.

"Just run. He told me I had to run or I'd fall."

Saint chewed viciously at her thumbnail. She wore a rather large diamond ring on a rather grubby ring finger. It looked peculiarly unfitting for the scruffy boy's garb. "Was he touching you? What did it feel like?"

"No, he wasn't. And, uh, I could feel I was treading on something. It went away if I stopped moving." Ben winced at the sudden, vivid memory of the foothold disappearing from under him. "He said we couldn't do it together. He went first and I ran to him. That's all I know."

Saint wore the kind of expression that would have made Ben's mother warn her about the wind changing. "Fuckin'ell," she muttered. "Prancing git."

"Jenny." Day spoke with weary rebuke.

"Yeah, but how the f— How the hell? I never knew anyone could do that. *I* can't do that. I want to know, Mr. D, that ain't normal."

"Ask him when we catch him," Day told her. "Although you'll have to talk quickly. We've received what I can only call an ultimatum from the Met, and giving them Pastern now will save us from making about fifty very unwelcome concessions. We're out of time. Spenser, you'll come with us."

They took a carriage to Regent's Park. Ben was to wait for Jonah in the gardens, and to lead him towards a certain path, where Day waited. Janossi would be in the gardens; Saint would be somewhere overhead.

"It will all be over after this," Day said, as Ben stared at his clasped hands. "You are doing the right thing. You know it. There's no choice."

They walked him into the gardens, then the justiciars disappeared. Ben went forward alone, to the bench he'd sat on before, and seated himself. It was still a few minutes to four.

The crocuses pushed through the earth in front of him, many of the flowers now in full bloom. They brought back the memory of the other day—was it just yesterday? It felt longer. He'd sat here, waiting for Jonah…

…who they were going to arrest, and hobble, because Ben had told them where to find him.

Giving Jonah up was the right thing to do. He knew, absolutely, that it was the right thing to do. There was no question of that. He was a criminal.

Ben looked down the path. A trim figure came towards him, lifting a hand in greeting. Ben could see Jonah's irrepressible pleasure in every quick stride, as he hurried towards his imprisonment, his betrayer.

Then he was on his feet, screaming. "Run, Jonah! They're here for you! *Run!*"

His voice was cut off as something seized him by the throat and an invisible blow landed in his stomach. He doubled over, winded, but he'd got the words out and Jonah, after one frozen fraction of a second, turned and sprinted. Behind Ben, Janossi bellowed a curse and pounded by, and Saint erupted from the trees, through the air, moving astonishingly fast. Jonah was already out of sight, and Ben flopped back down onto the bench, breathing hard, shaking.

After a few moments, he became aware of someone standing over him, and looked up, although not very far, to see Stephen Day.

"I suppose that was my fault." Day spoke in the calm, almost chatty tone he'd used to Janossi earlier, and it made the hairs rise on Ben's neck. "I quite underestimated your determination to ruin your life for the sake of the most worthless individual of my acquaintance. I told you, more than once, that giving him up was the right thing to do. Was I insufficiently convincing?"

"No." Ben stood. He towered over Day, but he didn't delude himself that gave him any chance at all. He thought he could feel a tension in the air around him: perhaps just his imagination, but he was quite sure that the invisible bonds would close round him again if he tried to run.

He had no right to run. He'd aided the escape of a wanted man. Committed a crime. He looked down at Day and went on. "No, you were right. He should be arrested."

"But you decided he wouldn't be."

"Yes."

Day stuck his hands in the pockets of an expensive topcoat, incongruously worn over a shabby and battered jacket. "Fine. Your decision, Spenser, although this leaves you facing the music on his behalf for the second time, and by God, you will face it now. Lost him, have we?" He didn't look round as Janossi panted up.

"Saint's after him," Janossi offered. "They're both in the air."

"Over Regent's Park." Day massaged the bridge of his nose. "Good. Marvellous. Do you think she's likely to catch him?"

"Pastern had a good start." Janossi cast an unkind look at Ben.

"My responsibility," Day said. "Right, well. Saint will return in due course, with or without that flying nuisance. I suggest we bring Mr. Spenser back to the cells and decide what to do with him there."

Ben did not want to go back to the red-brick building, to the strange people who worked there, or to another cell. "What's your authority?" he demanded. "You police magicians. I'm not a magician. Have you any right to detain me?"

"Good question." Day considered it, with a thoughtful air. "My authority… Well, for one, you're a practitioner's accomplice and I'm holding you as such. For another, by the terms of our agreement with the Met, I can hold unskilled criminals till they can be handed over. And for a third, if you argue with me now, I'll drag you by the neck till your bones snap. Does that clarify things?"

CHAPTER SIX

Ben spent a long time back in the little cell—and it was a cell, now, the door firmly locked, a chamber pot in the corner. He banged on the door a few times, at first experimentally, then trying to shake a rising fear that these odd, angry people might have forgotten his existence. Nobody came.

Some hours after he was put in there, the door was unlocked by Waterford, the pudgy youth with the broken nose. Ben felt the invisible force clamp around him as his gaoler entered, much harder than when Day had detained him. Waterford carried in a plate of stew and a jug of water, which he put on the table. He looked at Ben, said, "Bloody poof," and deliberately let a long string of saliva drool into the jug.

It wasn't the first time—the only question in the cells after Jonah's first escape had been whether he saw them spit or not. That didn't make it any easier to bear.

He drank the water anyway, because he was thirsty.

There was no bed. There was a blanket in the corner and, when it became apparent that he would not be moved that night, Ben arranged it over himself and settled to rest in the chair.

He spent a restive, uncomfortable night, thinking of Jonah, wondering if he'd made his escape. Jonah deserved arrest, he was well aware of that. Ben had, without doubt, been wrong to interfere with justice, and he had brought this latest disaster on himself. But Jonah had done things for Ben's sake too, and he harboured the knowledge of that in his heart like the last ember of a dying fire.

He tried not to think of what would happen to him in the morning. There was, he supposed, a chance that they might just let him go. He had a feeling his luck wasn't running that way.

He dozed fitfully and was wide awake, chill and bleary-eyed, by the time distant clocks struck five. Someone, thankfully not Waterford, brought him coffee and porridge, and he forced it down, then set himself to waiting.

At last the door opened once more, and Day slipped in, followed by the lumbering Mrs. Gold. She looked, if possible, even more pregnant than before. Ben stood to give her the chair, which she took with a nod of thanks.

"Spenser," Day said. "Did you sleep well?"

"Not really. And your man Waterford spits in prisoners' drinks. Just so you know."

Mrs. Gold made a face of unutterable weariness. "For heaven's sake. Steph, would you mind?"

"Of course. Excuse me." Day left the room. Ben waited for several minutes, not entirely sure what for. Mrs. Gold didn't speak, sitting with her eyes closed, seeming to enjoy the rest. Ben wondered if she was asleep, if there was any chance he could slip out.

"Don't try it," Mrs. Gold said, without opening her eyes.

Day came back in with a jug of water and a cup. "Here." He poured Ben a drink. "I've had a quick word with Waterford. Sorry about that, Spenser."

"He's going to have to get used to it," Mrs. Gold remarked.

"Quite." Day propped himself against the wall behind her. "We have an agreement with the Met, Spenser. We, practitioners, conduct ourselves discreetly, we govern ourselves to prevent magical crime affecting the rest of the population, and we ensure wrongdoers are punished. The Met were already furious at the dead officers and Pastern getting away scot-free. So it did not help when he and you windwalked out of a police raid on a molly house. And it *really* did not help that, yesterday, Pastern led Saint on an aerial chase all the way down Great Portland Street, over Oxford Street to Regent Street, and right through the Liberty Bazaar. That was not what they had in mind by discretion."

"In fairness, it's just as much Saint's fault as Pastern's," Mrs. Gold observed. "I told you she's grossly overindulged."

"You may argue with her fiancé about that," Day said. "I shouldn't dare. And if we're talking of fairness, Pastern made a damned good stab at destroying her life last winter. She's got a grudge against him, and I don't blame her for it. Though I do blame her for windwalking through Liberty's, yes," he added, as Mrs. Gold twisted round to give him a look. "In any case, the pair of them caused utter havoc, leaving us with an extremely angry police commissioner and a Council scrabbling for solutions, so…"

"So we're handing you over," Mrs. Gold told Ben.

"To whom?"

"The Met," Day said. "Who intend to prosecute you as Pastern's accomplice in the murders of four police officers."

"But that's nonsense," Ben said. "I was in gaol. I knew nothing of it."

"You've helped him escape justice twice. You're conducting a criminal liaison with him. If the Met can't get him, they're going to have you instead. You're a poor second, but you'll do."

"How is that fair?"

"I don't think fairness is the concern here," Mrs. Gold remarked dryly.

"I doubt the widows and orphans of the painter's victims think it's fair either," added Day. "You chose your side yesterday, now you can take the consequences. I have several practitioners in uncomfortable situations with the law right now, and a lot of trouble on the streets because of the lack of police co-operation. If handing you over is going to buy us back that co-operation, it's what we'll do." He shrugged. "I did tell you Pastern was a catastrophe. You should have listened."

"But…" Ben needed to think, but he felt as though he'd been punched in the stomach. He'd expected it to be bad, but a vengeful prosecution, as a policeman implicated in the murders of his fellows, a bent copper…

He'd thought the time he'd already served had been bad. He'd be lucky to survive this.

"This is justice, is it?" he managed.

"Your sort," Day said. "As you pointed out to me, you're not in my jurisdiction. I did try to help you."

"Leave it, Steph." Mrs. Gold stood, with some effort. "Let's get him ready. I'll send someone in with cuffs."

She waddled out. Ben sat, heavily, head in hands. He wondered if demanding a lawyer would do any good. As if he could afford one.

"You know this isn't right."

"I do, yes." Day sounded close to sympathetic. "But if we can't give them Pastern, they'll make do with you, and that's all. Were I you, I'd stop sacrificing myself for him." His eyes caught Ben's, oddly intent. "Really, Spenser. Don't sacrifice yourself for him again."

As if he'd have the chance. Ben had no idea what sort of term he might expect, but a vengeful judge who chose to name him accessory to murder could send him down for more years than he'd survive.

Waterford came in a few minutes later. He was white-faced and sweaty, and Ben wondered what Day's "quick word" had entailed. He cast Ben a look of intense dislike as he handed Day a rope.

"We can't afford handcuffs?" Day enquired.

"There's none in the cupboard, sir," Waterford muttered. "Anyway, he's not a practitioner."

"Oh, well, then. Stand with hands in front please, Spenser. I will make you," he added, not unkindly, when Ben didn't rise at once. "I'd rather not."

Ben stood, breathing deeply, and allowed Day to rope his wrists, which the man did with surprising deftness. Day walked with him to the main entrance, where three police constables waited. None of them made eye contact with him, their glazed expressions expressing their disdain.

"The prisoner Spenser," Day said. "You're taking him to Cannon Street, yes?"

"That's right, sir. Are you intending to come, sir?" There was a definite note of hostility in the constable's question.

"No, he's not a practitioner. I'm sure you can manage. Off you go." Day turned without a farewell and went back inside, as big hands closed on Ben's arms.

"Right, Margery." A harsh voice, breath hot and close on Ben's ear. "Get your arse in the carriage. There's a few people down the nick want a *word* with you."

It was a short drive to Cannon Street. Ben stared at the floor, not wanting to antagonise his guards by meeting their eyes or to give them an excuse to call him aggressive. He'd learned that much. He felt nauseous anticipation of what was coming.

Hell, hell, hell. Why had he called out? It could be Jonah here now, not him. Jonah, who'd left him before…

But in the end, it hardly mattered what Jonah had felt, how many lies there had been. Jonah had betrayed him, and Ben had betrayed him right back, but they had loved each other once, and Ben would take this punishment now in memory of that, because there was nothing else left for him to do.

That didn't make the prospect of what was coming any easier to bear.

The cab stopped. One of the constables stuck his head out of the window and pulled it back in with a scowl. "Some sort of disturbance outside the station. Nothing serious, it looks like. Let's go."

They stepped out of the carriage, police before and after Ben so that they could ensure he had no opportunity to bolt. He took a deep breath of the grimy air while he could, and looked around. Cannon Street was busy, with cabs rattling up and down, crowds of fast-striding office workers, flower girls and hawkers crying their wares. He could see the disturbance in front of the steps to the station door. A spilled barrow of herring, twinkling silver in damp heaps on the cobbles, a barrow of apples abandoned on the street, and a couple of enraged costers bellowing elaborate insults in each other's faces, watched by a large and appreciative crowd, as a policeman attempted to calm them.

"Right, let's get this one in," remarked one of Ben's guards, then gave a cry of fury as a fish flew out of the crowd and smacked his broad chest. There was a shriek of juvenile laughter from the crowd. "Hoi! Don't you—" More fish flew. "Oi! You pack that in!" Another policeman gave a bellow of anger, and suddenly it seemed as if the whole younger section of the crowd decided that a fish fight was needed. Sprats flew. The fishmonger gave a yell of protest and lunged at a child.

A pebble flew down, its trajectory just missing Ben's head, and rattled on the pavement at his feet. He looked up, instinctively, as another stone dropped. What damned fool…? Ben tilted his head back, and saw, silhouetted against the sky, the dark crouching shape of a man, hunched like a great black bird on the roof of the police station.

Jonah leaned forward, over the guttering, at an angle that made Ben's stomach seize. He beckoned, and made a sort of tiptoeing motion with his hands, which Ben realised was meant to be the action of walking up stairs. He stared, confused, then understood what Jonah meant.

There was a constable on each side of him, but their grips were slack as they watched the chaos in front of the station. If he told them Jonah, the true accessory to murder, was on the roof…

They wouldn't catch him. Jonah would get away, and Ben would show he was on the right side, retrieve a small part of his reputation. Jonah would see him do it, though, hear him, and he'd run and never look back.

And that would be best for them both. Jonah was the catastrophe Day had called him. He should do it. Anything else was madness.

Ben stared up. Jonah gestured, quick and urgent.

Day had told him not to sacrifice himself for Jonah again. Day, who had looked so much as though he wanted to help. In fact, Day had *warned* him…

"Oh no," Ben said under his breath, and charged up. He had no idea how to do this but he lifted a leg as though ascending an imaginary staircase, and felt the spongy support form under his foot, and then he was climbing frantically, great long steps, terrified of falling or a hand closing round his ankle, with furious cries erupting below. He scrabbled, desperate and terrified, up through the air to the rooftop where Jonah crouched, white-knuckled. Jonah grabbed for him, and Ben flung himself to the tiles, and jerked out, "Trap!"

Jonah yanked Ben to his feet and cursed as a shot spanged off the lead guttering. "Buggery! Come on." Ben jerked his bound hands, and Jonah whipped out a knife that severed the rope in a single slice. He grabbed Ben's hand, and they were scramble-running up the roof, over the ridge—

A small form flew at Jonah with a banshee screech.

He let go of Ben's hand and leapt, hurtling upwards, just avoiding the attack. Jenny Saint tumbled past, rolling and turning like a circus acrobat, and sprang upwards as Jonah crashed down on her from the air, feet first. They collided hard, Saint sending Jonah head over heels even as he landed on her, the impact knocking the breath out of both.

Ben, bereft of Jonah's hand and the magical pressure that kept him steady, scrabbled desperately for balance and fell sideways, getting a hand around the roof ridge. The tile he gripped shifted and gave, and he grabbed for another, sick with terror. That held, and he hauled himself up for a more secure grip on the chimneystack, watching the windwalkers as they both staggered back to their feet.

Saint was ready for action first. She lashed out with a spinning kick that looked more like ballet than fighting, but it caught Jonah in the chest with vicious force as he rose. He stumbled and fell again. She gave a triumphant yell, leaping at him, and Ben, still hanging on to the chimney, wrenched off the loose tile with his other hand and hurled it at her.

It caught her square on the side of the head. Ben felt a fraction of a second's intense satisfaction before he realised with abrupt horror that he'd assaulted a young woman and an officer of the law. She stumbled sideways, staggering, clutching her head, tripped on the gutter, and fell off the roof with a shriek.

"Fuck, fuck, *fuck*." Jonah was back by Ben, grabbing his hand. "We're going to die. Run." He tugged him along to the edge of the roof. "You first, straight over, hurry."

Ben leapt out, took three long strides and heard a volley of shots. He stopped, the instinct operating well before his brain, and the air went from beneath his foot. Jonah screamed something, and there was a hard shove under his flailing foot, but Ben wasn't running now, he was falling, and unlike Jonah he couldn't turn in midair.

Something crashed between his shoulder blades, pushing him forward into the brick wall that faced him, just as another shot went right by him. There was a buffeting sensation under his feet, keeping him up as he scrabbled for a grip on the brick, then a thump above him as Jonah hit the roof and hung down, arm outstretched, hand perhaps three feet from Ben's head.

"Jump!" Jonah yelled.

There were more shots. Cries from below. Ben braced himself against nothing and urged himself upwards. He found a hand clutching his, and Jonah somehow hauling and pushing him up.

"Run," Jonah gasped, as Ben rolled himself over the gutter onto the tiles. "Come on. Stay away from the edges."

There was nothing Ben wanted more than to stay away from the edges. There were men with guns down there, and probably practitioners, and his shoulder blades were prickling in anticipation of Miss Saint rising up in the sky like an avenging Cockney angel. Jonah kept twisting round as he ran, evidently with the same fear. They were on a long string of terraces now, though, house adjoining house, and out of sight of the people on the ground. Jonah sent Ben over a gap onto another, lower set of buildings, older ones, river-rotted with the damp of the nearby Thames, and they slipped and slid and stumbled together, with the great dome of St. Paul's rising high in the cityscape that faced them.

They ran and jumped and windwalked, till the cathedral was well behind them, until finally Ben's prison-bound legs, too long off the rugby pitch, were screaming their protests. Jonah gasped, "Breather." He pulled Ben down with him, nestling into a space between a crazy coppice of chimney pots, and ducked his head between his knees as Ben tried to fill his lungs with the salty, grimy air.

At last Ben panted, "Did we lose them?"

"We lost Saint. Which I think means she hurt herself, because that woman is fast. And if we're going to be blamed for that, we're in a lot more trouble now. A *lot*."

"That doesn't seem possible," Ben managed to point out. There were black spots in front of his eyes.

"It's always possible," Jonah said. "She has terrifying friends. Oh, damn it. I hope she's not dead."

That thought had been very much in Ben's mind too. "She's a windwalker. Surely…"

"No, I can get hurt falling off things as much as the next man, if I don't catch myself on the way down. But she's a tough one, she might have made it. Oh Lord." Jonah let his head flop back with a groan. "I do seem to make a mess of things. I had no idea the justiciary would be there."

"I was bait. Day more or less told me so. They knew you'd come for me."

"Did they?" said Jonah, and then, hesitantly, "Did you?"

Ben tried to steady his breathing, in and out. "Where are we going?" he asked, after a moment, and winced as he realised what he'd said. It came so naturally. "That is—should we split up?"

"No. We shouldn't." Jonah's eyes were on Ben's, intensely blue, and Ben gave a little nod, because the thought of running from retribution alone in this huge, unfriendly city held no appeal. That was, without doubt, the reason.

"Um...I don't know," Jonah said, going back to his question. "I think we should leave London as soon as possible, by which I mean when you have your breath back. Where... They might anticipate us going north, to Hertfordshire or Manchester. Doubling back east doesn't appeal. South or west, nowhere you have any connections, what do you think?" He shrugged at Ben's look. "If we don't have a destination in mind, they won't be able to guess it. Pick one."

"Southwest."

"Reading? Gloucester? Exeter, maybe? Why not. That's a train from Paddington, then."

"I don't have a ha'penny to my name." The realisation struck Ben with force. "My clothes, everything, it's all back at the dosshouse—"

"So it's gone. The police are going to be quite testy about this, you know, and the justiciary even worse. We can't go back."

"No—but—" Ticket fare. Something else to wear. Food.

"I'll deal with the money," Jonah said. "I have resources."

"I don't want your money." The words were out without Ben's conscious thought, a bursting of five months' resentment.

Jonah's eyes widened. "I wasn't proposing— Oh, goodness, Ben, I got you into this, could you not please let me try to get you out?"

"You didn't last time." Ben's voice rasped.

"No," Jonah said. "I had reasons for that, but…later?"

Later wasn't good enough. Ben wanted to know now, right now, why Jonah had abandoned him so utterly five months ago. Why there had been no attempt at contact in all that time. Why he had not been there, waiting at the prison gate for his release, as some tiny, contemptible part of Ben's soul had believed he would be, and been crushed at the absence.

On the other hand, they were running from the law.

"Later," he agreed. "But I need to know, Jonah. I need to understand."

"Everything, I promise. Once we get on a train."

CHAPTER SEVEN

They came down from the rooftops not long afterwards, to Ben's intense relief, losing themselves in the London crowds. He forged ahead, consumed with the need to reach the station. Jonah seemed less urgent, and less forceful, buffeted by the crowds, constantly managing to get in the way of the people who sidestepped Ben.

It took a good ten minutes for Ben to realise what was happening, and when he did he seized Jonah's arm with all the force of the avenging law he no longer represented.

"Are you picking pockets?" he hissed savagely.

"Ssh! Of course I am."

"Jesus Christ." Ben shook him. "You—"

"If we don't get out of London in the next few hours, either the police or the justiciary or Miss Saint's fiancé is going to catch up with us. And I didn't have any money. Now I do. We're on the run from the law, you can't quibble about a bit of fingersmithing."

"Yes, I can," Ben snarled back, aware that the low-voiced argument was attracting too much attention. "Stop it."

"How else are we going to get out of London?" Jonah demanded. "Beg for funds?" He held Ben's eyes for an answer he didn't have, shook off his grip and strode on.

It was a long walk. Long enough for Ben to start sweating every time a hurried footstep or a fast-moving hansom came up behind them, convinced that the Met or the justiciary must have caught up with them by now. Long enough for him to wonder what the devil he was doing, and why the devil he kept doing it.

He knew the answer. It was because of the devil who walked beside him.

He looked round, checking for pursuit, sweeping a quick glance over Jonah. He was silent, apparently thinking, features relaxed into their habitual expression of faint amusement. He smiled when he slept, Ben remembered, and the thought was a tiny adder-bite in his chest.

He knew how Jonah looked when he slept, and the sounds he made when he came, and the places to touch that made him writhe and beg. He knew that Jonah was ashamed that he could not read, shameless in his love of men. He knew that he liked his tea weak and his toast close to burned.

He didn't know anything important. He didn't know anything about Jonah's powers or his past or his criminal nature. He didn't know if Jonah had let other men have him in the last five months. He didn't know why they were running together, except that it felt a matter of instinct to do so, and he didn't know if that instinct was as self-destructive as every other instinct of his involving Jonah.

He knew about that torn, bloodstained pencil sketch that Jonah had protected at such appalling cost, and about Jonah perched on the rooftop of the police station, silhouetted against the sky…

"Did you organise that?" he asked. "At the station?"

"What, the costers? Yes." Jonah grinned round at him. "I thought they were rather good, didn't you? Particularly the fish."

"They caused a public nuisance," Ben said, and Jonah's smile faded at the note of heavy, sober reproof. Which was right because it was one more grossly irresponsible act to Jonah's discredit, but Ben found himself wishing he'd given in to the glimmer of a laugh he'd felt, the pale echo of the old lightheartedness. He stamped on a stupid urge to admit that it had, perhaps, been funny.

Instead, he asked, "How did you know I'd be there?"

"You won't approve if I tell you." Jonah sounded a touch sulky.

He probably wouldn't. And if Jonah hadn't done it, whatever it was, he'd be in a cell right now, and lucky if he was only being spat at.

"Thanks." The word jerked out awkwardly. "For coming, for getting me out of that."

"You warned me in the park," Jonah pointed out. "I couldn't just—" He stopped.

"Leave me to be arrested?"

Jonah pressed his lips together, staring at the pavement as they headed towards the station. "No. I couldn't have left you to that again. Come on, we're here. I'll get tickets if you get us some food for the journey." He produced a ten-shilling note. Ben glared at it. Jonah took his hand and shoved the note in. "Don't be like that. It's ours now, and starving won't help. Ben, you need to eat."

"I'd rather starve than thieve," Ben said, low-voiced. "Understand that, Jonah."

"Yes, well, understand *this*: if we get caught now, I'm not the only one who'll end up with broken bones." Jonah leaned in, hissing. "You've upset the Met and the justiciary, and when you lobbed a tile at that nuisance Saint, you made worse enemies than them both. If you care about tuppenny-ha'penny morals, there's a police station round the corner where you can hand yourself in. Otherwise, we're getting out of London with money that did not originally belong to me, but our need is greater than theirs, do you see?"

It was, in that moment, all too tempting to head for the police station. Ben clenched his fists. "No more of it. Once we're out of London, no more stealing."

"As you wish," Jonah snapped, in anything but an accommodating tone. "Meanwhile, let's get on a train, shall we?"

It wasn't just all the things done, and the things yet to be said lying between them, Ben realised. It was fear. He was so tightly tensed it hurt to move his shoulders, and though Jonah affected his usual casual stance, Ben knew that terror was gripping him too. The white girders of Paddington Station's roof arched over them in a metal spiderweb, and he had a sudden, appalling vision of the justiciar Saint perched above him, waiting to drop. He had to restrain himself from craning his neck to look up.

Instead he bought food with the stolen money, slabs of veal pie, buns and plum dough, and bottles of ale as well, and the serving girl did not hold up the note and cry him a thief. She grumbled about making change and found him a paper sack, and he met Jonah in the middle of the platform laden with spoils.

"There's a train to Gloucester leaving in fourteen minutes," Jonah announced. "So we're going there."

The train was not busy. To Ben's surprise, Jonah waved him into a second-class carriage, and an empty, comfortable compartment.

"Why aren't we travelling third?" he asked. "It's a waste of money, and I don't look—respectable."

"Leave that to me," Jonah assured him. "Really, it'll be—oh, bother." That was as the door opened and a fussy-looking man in a suit entered, putting his newspaper on the seat. Jonah smiled at him and leaned over to touch his hand as he said, clearly, "Now, listen, you don't want to sit in here." The man mumbled an awkward excuse and backed out, leaving the paper in his haste to get away.

"How did you do that?" Ben demanded. "Did you affect his thoughts?"

Jonah shrugged. "We need privacy."

"Yes, but—"

"But we need privacy. He can sit somewhere else."

"You can't just shape the world to your own convenience like that," Ben protested.

"What does it matter where he sits?—No, listen to me, you don't want to come in," Jonah added to a young man fumbling at the door. "Goodness, it's like Piccadilly Circus."

"It matters because…it's wrong, that's why."

"Oh, well, *wrong*," Jonah said dismissively.

"But—" Ben gave up, for the moment, and sat back in silence, until at last the train jolted away with a cloud of steam and a screech of metal. The ticket inspector came in a few moments later, and Jonah handed over the scraps of pasteboard.

"What's this, now?" demanded the inspector. "These are third-class—"

"Second class." Jonah's hand snaked out to the inspector's fingers. "Listen to me. Second class, and you don't need to disturb us, for any reason."

"Very good, sir." The inspector touched his cap and departed.

Jonah pulled the door closed. "Now, don't fuss. You were quite right about husbanding our money, especially if you're going to make difficulties about replenishing the funds."

"I'm happy to have third-class tickets and sit in third."

"I'm not," Jonah said. "It's uncomfortable, and we wouldn't get any quiet, and does it really matter?"

"It seems to me that it's all of a piece. You're not honest, Jonah."

Jonah's cheeks reddened, just a little, but he gave a careless shrug. "Perhaps not. Well, no. If you want to be provincial about it."

"I am provincial," Ben said grimly. "I'm a provincial copper, or I was, till a few months ago. And if you've got an explanation of why I'm not one any more, I'd like to hear it now. No excuses, no wandering off the point." He knew Jonah's flitting, butterfly mind all too well. "Just the truth."

Jonah shut his eyes. "Yes. Right. Very well. Where to start… I don't know if you remember, no reason you should, but back in October, before…everything, I turned down a job."

Ben did remember. Jonah had come back from one of his two-day absences twitchy and frowning. He had said only that he had refused work, and the prospective employer had not been happy, but he had scowled at his plate as he ate, and his normally ravenous appetite had deserted him. Ben had wondered at the time.

"Let me guess. This job offer was from Lady Bruton?"

"Yes. A very bad woman, and very dangerous, and half-mad at least, and possessed of a raging grudge against Stephen Day, the justiciar, and his lover, Lord Crane."

"His *what*?"

"Lover. Day's lover."

"Day?" Ben repeated, completely forgetting about sticking to the point. "His lover? Did you say a *lord*?"

"Oh, yes. The right noble earl of Crane. Landed gentry. Six foot three of money, mouth and cock. And an utter bastard."

"Six— With Day?" Ben was having trouble visualising this. "Are you sure?"

"Unlikely, isn't it? And, you'd think, physically unfeasible, but they are conducting an *affaire* of operatic intensity. No, really. I promise." His eyes brimmed with amusement at Ben's reaction.

"But... My *God*. I thought he was sympathetic." Ben considered it for a second. He had a vague feeling that, under the circumstances, the man might have been more helpful. "Well, I wouldn't have thought it."

"Yes, well, think on this: the righteous Mr. Day is quite a lot less righteous in private. He likes *restraints*."

"You aren't serious," Ben said, aghast. "Oh."

"What?" Jonah was watching his face, and there was something in his expression, a touch of satisfied happiness that he had always worn when he made Ben laugh. The look that had made Ben feel like the centre of the world. "What is it?"

Ben didn't give a damn for Day's personal habits, but that look had made him feel...he didn't know. Something he couldn't think about. He answered mostly to distract himself from it. "Nothing. Just that you said restraints, and—well, I thought Day was good at ropes back at the justiciary..."

"No!" Jonah said with explosive glee. "Oh my God, Benedict Spenser. You let Stephen Day tie you up. You *tart*."

"I didn't *let* him, he arrested me," Ben protested, which was the wrong thing to say. He should have slapped Jonah down. They weren't on these terms any more. But they had been, and it felt so natural, so alive. "Anyway, I don't believe a word of it."

"God, well, nor did I. Who would? You've seen Day, whereas his lordship's absolutely delectable, if you like that sort of thing—"

"Do you?" Ben found himself interrupting, with hostility.

Jonah's eyes came swiftly to Ben's, a distinct glow to them. "Well, if you ask me, he's a bit Blackpool, you know. Nice for a holiday, but you wouldn't want to live there."

"You're ridiculous." Ben had to hold back the smile. He wanted to laugh, wanted so much to have Jonah spin his implausible gossip and make the world a lighter, easier place.

He didn't want to stop this and talk about awful things, and for just a moment he thought, *Perhaps we could not.* Just forget. Just ignore. Just have a few minutes on the train where the past wasn't with them, where he could inhale Jonah's scent and maybe even sit by him instead of apart. Feel the warmth of his thigh against Ben's, have Jonah's fingers tangle in his own, perhaps even, when the train passed through a tunnel and all was dark, he could steal a kiss and things could be as they had been once more...

Insanity. Sheer bloody insanity.

Ben stamped down on the little bubble of happiness, and Jonah saw him do it. The smile stayed on his lips, but the light left his eyes, and he was already nodding as Ben said, heavily, "Come on."

Jonah took a deep breath. "Yes. Right. Where was I?"

"Lady Bruton. The job."

"Well. She told me that she wanted me to work for her. She needed me to steal, incriminate Miss Saint, and get a ring of some value from Day. It was all aimed at him, you understand. Another operatic sort of person, Lady Bruton. I said no. She said I'd do as I was told, or she'd make me." He made a face. "She was frightening. Half-mad, horribly disfigured, consumed by revenge, far, far stronger than me, and she didn't take no for an answer. That was why I did the Tring Museum job, you see. It fell into my lap—obviously it did, it was a trap—but at the time it seemed like a marvellous opportunity to make a lot of money very quickly. Because I thought we might have to run, you and me."

"You never told me that."

"'Darling, I can walk on thin air and a warlock is trying to make me steal a magic ring,'" Jonah mimicked. "No. I didn't say anything. I still hoped I could make it go away. It was stupid of me, but I didn't want it to touch you. And then I did the job, and you were there." He was staring out of the window as he spoke. "I didn't mean that to happen."

"How could it not?" Ben asked. "I'm—I was a policeman."

"I don't know. I don't plan very well, Ben. I just…run, really. Keep on going and try to stay a bit ahead." He took a deep breath. "But Lady Bruton was so far ahead of me. I never had a chance. I got away from the museum, that night, and I doubled back and went home—"

"*I* went home," Ben said furiously. "You never came back."

"Oh, I did. I came back long before you could have and found Lady Bruton in the sitting room, and… She made me come with her. Dragged me to some barn in the middle of a field, and there was this man there, Newhouse. The painter. He had a cat." Jonah swung back to Ben, eyes blazing. "He'd done a picture. And she held me to a chair and made me watch while he changed it. He took off its legs, and he did things to its eyes and—oh Jesus, Ben, it took hours. Hours. He wouldn't stop. That was why we were in a barn, so nobody heard the screaming. And halfway through, they, uh, they showed me… He'd sketched you. It was a good picture. I don't know how he got it—"

"There was an artist, back at the station, in September. He said he was illustrating a novel."

"They'd planned it all." Jonah's shoulders were slumped, defeated. "God knows how far in advance. We never had a chance, did we? Anyway, they showed me they had you, and then he went to work on the cat again, until I said, yes, I'll do whatever you tell me, and Lady Bruton smiled at me, and she said, 'I know.'"

"God. But—"

"I wanted to tell you," Jonah overrode him. "Say goodbye. I begged her to let me, and she said I could, but I had to meet them in Hemel Hempstead at noon on Thursday. This was Tuesday night. She said I could have a day, but Newhouse would start work on your picture at noon on Thursday if I wasn't there. And that would have been fine, except for the bloody justiciary."

"They were on your tail."

"Yes, they were," Jonah said resentfully. "They caught up with me Wednesday afternoon. I got away, just, but I was running all night. I didn't want to lead them to you. I shook them off eventually and lay low in the timber yard. By then I'd realised that the important thing was to get to Hemel Hempstead in time, even if I didn't see you, so I was going to have a couple of hours' rest and get over there. But the sods found me." He shuddered. "I fought, Ben, really I did. It was Thursday morning. I knew what was going to happen at noon. I've never fought so hard in my life. But I lost, and they got me down, and then…"

"The carriage."

"I told you," Jonah whispered. "I said you had to let me go. I didn't know what to do."

"You could have told me something," Ben said. "Surely. You could have trusted me—"

"But you didn't trust me. I was a thief who'd lied to you for months. If I'd started babbling about you being in danger— And it was eleven o'clock, Ben, I heard the bells, I had to get miles over open ground… So I did it. You know what I did."

"Did you use magic on me?" Ben's voice was thick and gritty. "To make me kiss you?"

Jonah's smile was painfully sad and twisted. "I tried, but I had iron on me, it stops the power. So I don't think it worked. I think that was just us, Ben. Just you."

Ben tried to speak. He couldn't find words.

"But I tried to," Jonah said. "And I left you there, on your own, and you went to prison for it, and I am sorry, Ben, so sorry, but… I got to Lady Bruton three minutes before noon, and you weren't dead."

There was a long silence. Jonah was breathing hard. Ben found it hard to breathe at all.

"Then?" he managed.

"Two months working for the Bruton bitch." Jonah tipped his head back, contemplating the ceiling of the compartment as the train rattled along. "Newhouse tore your picture at the edges every so often, to keep my mind on the task in hand. So I stole and impersonated and carried messages, and helped them kill policemen and entrap justiciars. I did try to get out. I even talked to Day, but it didn't go very well. I don't like justiciars, and they don't like me, and I was so angry all the time, it felt as though I was going mad. And mostly I couldn't *say* anything. I wasn't allowed to tell anyone about the painter, you see. Bruton would fluence me every now and then, and ask me questions, and if they found out I'd talked about him, they'd have killed you. Day was no help, and I couldn't think of anywhere else to turn, so I just kept doing what I was told, right up to the end."

"How did it end?"

"Oh, God, it was horrible. Newhouse had done a sketch of Crane, and they used that threat to capture Day. Then I had to fetch Crane so Lady Bruton could use Day to threaten him. Turn and turn about. She had it all worked out but…" He shuddered. "That man, Crane, he frightens me. He seemed to plan everything in the time it takes me to decide what to have for luncheon. He brought down the whole gang of them, all practitioners. Decapitated one with his bare hands."

"That isn't possible," Ben said, hoping he was right.

"Maybe not, but I saw him do it. I tell you what, there's something really *odd* about him. Anyway, he took the man's head off, and his henchman, who is the most appalling brute, cut the painter's throat. So all I had to do was be sure your picture could no longer hurt you, and then I ran like the devil was at my heels, because he was."

"Why didn't you stay?" Ben demanded. "Explain yourself? You were acting under duress, Day must have seen that. Surely he'd have understood you were forced to it."

"Maybe I should have." Jonah looked rather awkward. "The problem was, I didn't know if the power to hurt lay in the painter or the painting. Whether only Newhouse could rip the sketch and kill you, or if anyone could. So even when Newhouse was dead, I didn't know if you were safe. And I didn't know where your picture was, and Lady Bruton was still fighting, with Day in iron, and I had no reason to suppose Crane could beat her, and I wasn't going to help him if that risked you. It was an impossible situation. I didn't have any choice."

Ben had a distinct sense of impending doom. "What did you do?"

"I tore up Crane's picture."

"Tore…"

"The painter had it in his hand," Jonah explained. "And I thought, if I tore it and it didn't kill him, that would prove *you* were safe. So I did."

"Did Day see you do that?" Ben asked, without much hope.

"Both of them. Day and Crane. And, uh, I tore it a bit enthusiastically. It was all rather tense. If you must know, I ripped it in half, but it was fine, Crane didn't die. There's no point putting your face in your hands like that. There was a pitched battle going on and people being killed left, right and centre, and Saint had kicked me in the head which really hurt, so I'd have liked to see you handle it better. Oh, be reasonable."

"Do you think Day's going to be reasonable about it?" Ben enquired through his fingers.

"It's not Day I'm frightened of. Crane's a sod, and his pet murderer would cut my throat without blinking and *he*…this isn't very good, Ben…he's going to marry Saint."

"Saint," Ben repeated. "Miss Saint, who I knocked off a roof."

"I'm sure she's fine."

"So, we're now on the run from the justiciary, the Metropolitan Police, a rich and ruthless man that you tried to kill, and the extremely dangerous fiancé of the woman that *I* tried to kill. Is that right?"

"'Tried to kill' is overstating it," Jonah objected. "It's more 'might have accidentally killed, but didn't'."

Ben let his head drop back against the seat. "God almighty. Day was right. You're a catastrophe."

"You don't have to stay." Jonah hunched up, face darkening. "You can have the money I stole and get off at the next stop. They want me, not you."

"They want both of us. Trust me, Jonah. I've upset Day and the Met as much—well, not as much as you but quite enough."

The train rattled on.

"I've made a mess of this, haven't I?" Jonah sounded defeated. "I kept thinking I could keep going and find a way out. I couldn't let Newhouse kill you, and I couldn't let you go back to prison. But every time I've just got you in more trouble. God, Ben, maybe you should go. I'm not doing you any good."

"I looked for you when I came out," Ben said. "When they let me out of prison, part of me thought you'd be there. Waiting."

"I didn't even know you were inside." Jonah gave him a miserable smile. "How could I have? I can't read, I can't write, and even if I hadn't been slaved to Lady Bruton, I couldn't have shown my face in Hertfordshire to look for you. Eventually, when it was all over, I found someone I trusted to ask some questions for me, and that was when I learned that you'd been gaoled. I came back to London because…well, because I thought you might want to find me."

"I did. I wanted to wring your neck."

"I know. I don't blame you. If you still do, I'll understand. I don't mean I'll let you," Jonah added quickly. "Just that I'll understand if you want to."

Ben sighed. "No. No, I don't. Day showed me the picture." Jonah looked up, startled. Ben shrugged. "I wanted to hear your side. But he told me you'd been trying to save me. They do know that."

Jonah cocked his head, the familiar birdlike motion. "Do you think that means they might be a little more sympathetic?"

"No."

"I suppose not. Is that why you warned me in the park, because you knew about the picture?"

"Yes. Maybe." Was it? "I…I don't know. I told them where you were, after they told me all that. I helped them set that trap."

"You mean, Day fluenced you?"

"No. I wanted them to catch you."

"Oh." Jonah hunched his shoulders. "Well. Why did you—"

"I don't know."

They stared helplessly at each other, across the compartment, across the chasm between them.

"What are we going to do, Jonah?" The question came out without planning, propelled by Ben's confusion and unhappiness. "What now?"

"I don't know." Jonah gave him a hopeful flicker of a smile. "Could we, well, is there a way for us to start again, do you think? Not now, I don't mean that, but when you're ready—"

"We can't start again." Ben said that too loudly and gave a hasty glance at the closed compartment door, knowing this could not be overheard. "*We* never started in the first place, because you were lying to me the whole time." He felt a stab of irrational guilt at the slight sag in

Jonah's shoulders, and spoke a little more gently. "You're not the man I thought you were. And even if you were, I'm not the man I used to be."

Jonah huddled on the seat opposite. "Does it not…does it not count at all that I was doing those things with Lady Bruton for you? Doesn't that matter?"

"It matters." It mattered so much. One of the iron clamps round Ben's heart had loosened ever since he'd seen that pencil sketch of his own face, a dreadful thorny knot untangling at last. "I understand why you left me. I—God, Jonah. I hated you so much, for so long, and now I know you were thinking of me, you cared—" He stopped, voice suspended, hand over his eyes.

"Ben." Jonah sprang close to him, hand out, hovering. "Ben, listen—"

"No." Ben forced control on his voice. "Because, if you weren't a thief, it wouldn't have happened."

"It would," Jonah insisted. "Lady Bruton needed a windwalker, she'd have come and got me."

"But you wouldn't have been arrested first. I wouldn't have been there at all. You could have appealed to the justiciary. I could have helped you. Don't you see that?"

Jonah made a strangled noise, shoved himself back onto the opposite bench and turned away, staring out of the window as the train slowed, entering Reading Station. Drifts of steam rolled past the glass. "All right. Fine. It's all my fault, I brought it on myself. I know. Well, what now? You get off the train, and go and live your life somewhere else? Doing what?"

"I don't know. It doesn't matter. We're bad for each other," Ben said. "You lied to me. I betrayed you."

"You didn't." Jonah spoke urgently, trying to make it true, or to make it better, eyes wide with sincerity. "Ben, you did *not*."

And that, suddenly, was it. Too much. Far more than Ben could bear. "I can't do this any more. I'm going."

"Ben?" Jonah asked, bewildered, and then, "Ben!" as he stood, jerkily, and pushed his way out of the compartment.

No more. No more of the misery in Jonah's face, his uncomprehending, stubborn hope. No more of the ridiculous longing to kiss it away and make him happy again, or to bury his face in Jonah's chest and lose his own misery in the warmth and scent of him. No more being dragged from disaster to disaster in the wake of Jonah's chaotic, irresponsible progress—because he would be, he could feel the pull that made him want to stop thinking once more and slip back into happy, false, lethal ignorance to the sound of Jonah's laughter. No more of any of it, because it all hurt too much to be borne, and the thing that hurt the most was to know that Jonah wanted to spare him pain.

CHAPTER EIGHT

Ben blundered off the train, not looking forward or back. He shoved his ticket at the inspector, made his way blindly out into the unfamiliar town, and, with no idea where to go or what to do now, began to walk. Long strides, moving without thinking, trying to outpace the storm of memory and unhappiness and wishing that raged through him, and failing.

After a while, he wasn't sure how long, he stopped for a rest. He was hungry, he realised. He should have eaten something on the train—

That was when Ben realised that he was destitute.

Jonah had the stolen money, and the food they hadn't eaten. Ben had nothing in his pockets—he searched them now, to be sure, hoping for a few pennies, but they were empty. He had nothing to sell, having pawned his watch months back. He knew nobody in this town. The train was long gone. He was alone.

Ben stood, staring blankly, trying to understand what he'd done to himself and to think what to do now. There would be a workhouse, if he could beg for a place, but that was a last resort for desperation. He was able-bodied, strong still. Surely he could find a few pennies' worth of labour.

There was a policeman on the street corner. Ben plucked up his courage against the shame of poverty and went over to him.

"I beg your pardon, Constable. I'm looking for work. Can you tell me—"

"No begging, no soliciting." The constable folded his arms.

"I'm not begging," Ben said, as evenly as possible. "I want to work, and I don't know this town. If you can tell me where to go—"

"I said, no begging." He was a big man, and he leaned down over Ben with an officious loom, taking in his dishevelled, dirty clothes, the ugly scar. "Are you a vagrant?"

Vagrancy was a legal offence. To have no home and no money, while being able-bodied, made Ben a criminal by his very existence, one of the undeserving poor. He knew that well enough; he'd picked up plenty of men for it in his time.

"I'm not a vagrant," he said stubbornly. "I've somewhere to stay. I just want to find work."

"Well, you'd better get on and look, hadn't you?" the constable told him. "Because it's three of the clock now, and if I find you loitering after dark..." He gave Ben a significant look, leaned back and returned to doing nothing on a street corner.

Ben's hands were shaking as he walked off. He'd have liked to believe that the man was just a single bully, but he doubted it. The parish funded the workhouses, and they would have made their feelings known to the local force. This would not be a sympathetic town.

He looked. He did his best, asking anywhere that looked likely with more and greater urgency, but it was too late in the day, and he was filthy and unshaven after the night and the rooftop escape. Five refusals turned to ten, and twenty. He sounded more and more frantic as the gnaw of hunger turned painful, and his need repelled anyone who might have helped. There were enough willing men out there; nobody had to trust in a desperate one.

A few long, humiliating hours later, Ben was standing on the town bridge, stomach as empty as his heart, staring into the dark water below.

This would be a cold and hungry night, at best. There were no beggars huddled up under the bridge, which probably meant that he'd be moved on, or arrested, or beaten, if he tried to sleep there. They would have somewhere to go; there were always beggars. But Ben had no idea where they would be, where to go for a safe place to sleep, how to ask. He had no idea what he would do tomorrow.

The icy wind slashed through his thin coat. Beneath him the river water was swift, turbid, sweeping everything away in its rapid passage. It would sweep him away as quickly.

Every part of this, he had brought on himself. Every choice, every action and reaction, every decision to do with Jonah had led him to this place, and the worst of it was, all he could think about was Jonah's face as he'd walked out of the compartment, and the lost, abandoned expression in his eyes.

He wished he had said he was sorry, that would have been only decent. He should have said goodbye.

The wind whipped at his hair. Ben rested his arms on the cold iron of the railings, bowed his head and tried to find the strength for one last act.

A deep voice cut through the quiet. "Oi! You. You, there."

Ben looked up, a slight movement of vague curiosity, and saw the police constable from earlier, with another copper by his side. They came hurrying over, bull's-eye lanterns in hand. Perhaps they thought he might run. That wouldn't happen. He turned and stared back over the river, too weary to care any more.

"Oi," repeated the constable. "What's your name?"

God, did they have to go through this? "Spenser."

"Spenser?" The constable's voice betrayed eagerness. He lifted his lantern, shining the light on Ben's face, the distinctive scar. "Benedict Spenser. That's right, ain't it?"

Of course, Ben thought wearily, through the greyness. Of course the justiciary had followed somehow, traced them to Paddington and on from there. People had doubtless remembered a scarred man and another with a streak in his hair. The Met would have telegraphed to stations on the line. Of course they had. Of course Ben could not have escaped the consequences of his acts. Nobody ever did.

"Yes," he said drearily. "That's me."

"Told you, din't I?" the constable said to his colleague, with satisfaction. "I told you I saw him, and now we've got him. Feather in my cap, that'll be. All right, Spenser. You're going to come with us, now, sunshine. No trouble, understand?"

Ben couldn't summon up the strength to move. It didn't matter; they'd take him anyway. A cell, a train, back to the vengeful Met or the justiciary. He wondered vaguely, as if tackling a problem of logic, whether he could vault the railings and jump, but there was no resistance left in him.

"I said come with us. Right now." The big man's threat was clear: Ben would obey or be made to. His hand closed hard around Ben's upper arm, jerked roughly.

"You really shouldn't do that," said Jonah.

Ben's eyes snapped open. He swung round, disbelieving, but there he was, a few yards away: Jonah, hatless and windswept.

He didn't look at Ben. His attention was fixed on the two constables, and Ben had never seen him look as he did now. There was a wildness about him, a feral anger in his face, a quivering readiness to strike.

This was the Jonah Pastern who lied and stole and sent others to their deaths. This was Jonah fighting.

"No need to interfere, sir," began the second copper, but the first had sucked in a breath, staring at Jonah's piebald hair. He nudged the speaker, said as quietly as he could, "It's the other one," and cleared his throat.

"Best if you both come along with us, I reckon."

"Do you?" Jonah asked, with wide-eyed over-sincerity that made Ben's skin prickle. He took one light, almost dancing step forward, body taut with coiled power under pressure. "You think that's best? How sweet of you, thinking of us. You're *lovely*."

"Jonah," Ben said. "Don't hurt them."

"Would I?" Jonah's grin was all teeth. "Would I do that?"

"I mean it. *Don't.*"

The second policeman retreated a step. Ben didn't blame him. "Now, you listen—"

"Let go of him."

The policeman's grip on Ben's arm tightened. He began, "This man is under arrest," and Jonah moved. Not the spring of a fighter, leading with a knife or a punch, but an acrobatic leap, bouncing off the air, spinning, and landing a booted foot squarely in the man's face, so hard Ben heard the crunch of cartilage. The big copper went staggering down and back, letting go of Ben in his shock. The second, with panicked courage, lunged forward, and Jonah vaulted right over the top of the six-foot man's head, came down on the other side, thrust a foot between his legs and sent him stumbling forward over his colleague. As the two coppers tried to regain their feet, Jonah was over them, hands slapping on each man's neck.

"Listen to me." Jonah's eyes were burning blue in the moonlit darkness, his voice savage. "You don't know who we are. You don't know what happened here. You don't want him, and you don't want me. What you know is...you need to run. You need to run now, because there is something on this bridge that is going to rip you apart if you don't. Your worst nightmares are right here, waiting for you, coming for you, if you don't run *now*. Go!"

The constables broke, scrabbling to their feet with sobs of fear, and ran, boots pounding on the bridge. Ben stared after them, back at Jonah. He was watching the fleeing policemen, face startlingly grim. The magpie streak of his hair shimmered in the moonlight, white against black. Ben had always loved the mobility of his face, the vivid life of it, even when Jonah's rapid flitting from thought to thought had driven him to laughing distraction. Now he saw a stranger, still and intent and ruthless, with powers he didn't understand, and he was frightened.

"Uh," he managed.

Jonah looked round with quick concern, the implacable look dissolving as though it had never been. "Are you all right?"

"Why are you here?" Ben blurted out.

"You went away. You walked off and left me on my own—both of us on our own—and I got about three miles out of Reading and decided, I don't care." Jonah took a step closer. "I don't care if you don't love me now, or if you never love me again. I'm not going to leave you alone, and that's all there is to it. Let's just *go* somewhere." It was a plea. "There's a train going west at half past nine. We'll sneak onto it and go where it takes us, and go somewhere else from there, and stop when we've gone as far as we can. And I promise I don't expect you to forgive me, or anything else. But I'm so tired of not being with you. Come with me. Please?"

"We're not good for each other," Ben repeated, mostly to himself. He had to hold on to that, he knew, though he wasn't sure why any more, or what it meant.

"Perhaps not," Jonah said. "But we're not doing very well apart."

"I don't know. I don't know anything." Suddenly, Ben felt as though he could barely stand. He sagged back, using the parapet for support. "I— Oh, God, I'm so tired. I don't know what to do."

Jonah was in front of him then, pulling Ben forward, and he let his head flop onto the strong shoulder because he could no longer hold it up. "So come with me till you do know. You can change your mind when you're ready, but for now—" His hands gripped Ben's upper arms, holding him up as much as anything, because the exhaustion and despair had sapped all Ben's strength, and it was as much as he could do to hold back weak, hopeless tears. "Jesus Christ, Ben, my Ben, what happened? What did they do to you? Come on, lover. With me. We're going together."

CHAPTER NINE

Two days later they were in Cornwall.

They had been quiet most of the way, or at least Ben had. At first he'd been silent and numb, unable to think, his brain hopelessly fogged by confusion and uncertainty and the accumulated miseries of the last few days and months. Jonah hadn't tried to talk about them, or the future, or anything serious. He had passed Ben food that he ate like an automaton, and chattered in his inconsequential way, about rugby and old gossip, the weather and fellow passengers, a meaningless accompaniment that Ben listened to or ignored as his thoughts wandered. He had slept for what seemed like most of the journey, on railway carriage seats or hard benches, unconcerned by his safety because, he realised afterwards, Jonah was watching over him.

Then, that morning, waiting at a station, Jonah handed him an earthenware mug of tea, and Ben woke up.

"Uh. Thank you." He wrapped his hands around the mug, inhaling the steam that rose through the bright, chilly morning air.

"Morning." Jonah gave him a quick, lurking smile. "Welcome back."

"I…" Ben blinked. "Sorry. I feel like I've been asleep for days."

"You have. But not snoring. It's one of your most attractive qualities, you know, you never snore. Rare and precious, and"—his voice dropped, though they were alone on the platform—"sadly underrated in a bed partner. Not that I'm implying it's your best quality in that department, just that I appreciate it greatly."

"Idiot." Ben hid behind the cup, not sure of his own reaction. Jonah hadn't shaved for a couple of days, and the beginnings of a black beard gave him an air that Ben could only call piratical. He would look rather good with a well-trimmed beard, Ben thought, and then he was imagining the feel of that wiry hair against his own skin, the whisper of roughness it would bring to a kiss.

He had been lost in turmoil for so long, until that strange period of mindlessness and sleep. Now he felt awake, and alert, and with it, painfully aware of Jonah. His laughing eyes, and his mouth made for kissing, and the life that ran through him, always so bright and vivid, and that lithe strength that could knock Ben on his back…

He took a scalding gulp of tea. "Where are we?"

It turned out the trains had taken them to Exeter, and from there to Liskeard, where they were waiting for a train to somewhere called Looe.

"I said we'd go as far as we could, and this is about it," Jonah said. "I think after this we walk, or possibly ride a cow."

A tiny engine pulled two carriages along the coastal route to Looe, over steep inclines and through thick woods. From Looe a carter accepted a penny to take them further on, up the next cliffs, past Polperro, jolting along deep-sided narrow twisting lanes. They hopped out of the cart at a crossroads, where the carter was to go inland, and the little sea road ran down to a tiny fishing village. It was visible some way ahead, cottages spilling along the steep side of a deep cleft in the coastline.

"Just Pellore down 'ere," the carter warned them. His speech was so thick, it was hard to make out the words. "Not much doin' yerr."

"It sounds perfect," Jonah assured him.

They walked along the road in silence. The air was salty, bright with the scents of thyme and gorse.

"What are we going to do in a fishing village?" Ben asked at last.

Jonah shrugged. "Fish?"

"Do you know how?"

"No. Do you think it's difficult?"

"Extremely, I'd have thought." Ben had never been to Cornwall before, never seen the sea, in fact. He'd been watching the shifting blue sparkle all day, whenever he could, fascinated and a little unnerved. He hadn't quite understood how large it was. "I imagine people have to work hard round here."

"I can work hard," Jonah said, answering the unspoken question. "At least, I expect I can. It's never come up."

The long journey had sadly depleted their stolen funds, so finding some kind of work would soon become necessary. They were both travel-stained, luggageless, with nothing more than a pocketful of coins and the clothes they stood up in. But the sea was glittering in Ben's vision, the air was as clear and as intoxicating as gin, and Jonah was with him, shoulder to shoulder, stride by stride. In this moment, they were free.

The sun was already low over the sea, spreading a long golden pathway over the waves.

"We should think about a place to sleep at some point," Jonah remarked. "There's an inn there."

It was a large building, larger than one might have expected for such a remote place, perched at the top of the cliff where the road began its meander down to Pellore. Its whitewash was stained with sand and salt, and the grey slate roof had a disorder to it. A faded sign showed it to be the Green Man.

"Let's try the village first," Ben suggested. "See where we are and if we want to stay here."

It wasn't much. Pellore was a small agglomeration of cottages, huddled against the sea winds, running down a steep, narrow valley to a long stone quay that jutted into the sea, out past black bunched rocks.

Red-sailed boats were moored along the quay, and blue-jerseyed men in heavy boots moved with bent backs among piles of wet and stinking netting. The stone underfoot glimmered with damp and fish scales. A crab lay, belly up, legs flopped wide. Jonah took a step forward to inspect it, and hopped back, startled, as a mad-eyed seagull swept down with a flurry of wings to claim the treasure.

There was no way on earth that Jonah belonged here. What had they been thinking?

And there was no work, either. It was a fishing village, that was all, supporting itself, and nobody had any need for two rootless, shabby, ignorant Londoners. They walked around for a while, garnering too much attention, and as dusk fell, they set back up the road.

"This won't work," Ben said.

"Here won't," Jonah agreed. "Well, we've gone too far, that's all. We need a town. Let's stay here tonight and pick somewhere to head for tomorrow." He glanced over. "It'll be fine, Ben. The justiciary won't be able to alert every police force in every town in England. They won't even want to, I bet, they'll just want us—me—to go away."

Ben wasn't convinced of that. "What if Saint's dead?"

"I'm sure she's not. But if she is, it's too late for us to do anything about it. Come on. I want a drink, and a wash, and an actual bed."

"Can we afford that?" Ben said. "That is, we can't afford that."

"Yes, we can." Jonah spoke firmly. "This is a good thing to spend money on."

"Not if we don't have any."

"Don't worry about money, Ben. We'll manage."

"I told you," Ben said. "I won't live by stealing. No more theft."

"Yes, you said—"

Ben grabbed his arm, pulling him round. "Said it and meant it. I won't have it. If we're travelling together, or—or whatever we're doing, you can't steal. I want your word that you won't." What was that worth? "Your word to me."

Jonah exhaled hard. "I don't see why—well, obviously, I do see, but God, Ben, is this the time for moral scruples?"

It was exactly the time, when the broad and easy path beckoned so temptingly. "Yes. We'll find something else."

"Like you did in Reading? Surely if we need—"

"It's not about need. Everybody needs. You can't break the law because you *need*."

"We did, for months."

"That—" *That's different*, Ben wanted to say, but it wasn't. "All right, yes, but that harmed nobody else. The point is, I won't live by stealing and I don't want you to be a thief."

"Oh." Jonah looked startled. "Oh. I didn't think of it like that. Uh…" He gave Ben a glance that was almost shy. "If that matters to you…"

"Yes."

Jonah cocked his head. "All right. No more stealing."

"I mean it, Jonah. I want your word."

Jonah gave him a cheerful grin. "You have it. I give you my word." That didn't sound remotely like a serious decision and Ben was about to protest when Jonah waved a hand. "Anyway, you're doubtless right. We'll find something else easily enough."

"Will we?"

"Pfft. I've done plenty of this—"

"Running from the law?"

"Having nothing in my pockets and nowhere to go. The trick is not to weigh yourself down. Live through today the best you can and don't worry about tomorrow."

"Keep running, or you'll fall?"

"Exactly." Jonah gave a satisfied nod. Ben stopped and stared at his back as he trotted up the hill, wondering how to say, *You do realise that's how you dragged us both into this awful bloody mess in the first place?*

The Green Man was in shadow when they made it back up the steep hill. Lights flickered through the small-paned windows. Ben pushed open the thick, black-painted door, and they went in.

It was a very old inn. The floor was rough and uneven stone. A fire smoked badly in the huge hearth, not drawing properly, suggesting why the heavy beams and rough walls were so smoke blackened. A rather grim-looking landlady, her angular face lined with tiredness, turned as they approached the bar, and took in their unkempt appearances with a look of surprise that quickly changed to distrust. They were dusty, crumpled, and neither had shaved in days. Jonah's dark chin was on the way to respectable growth; Ben looked like the vagrant he was.

Jonah beamed at her, a wide, innocent smile that made her lips curve in instinctive response, before the stern expression returned. "Can I help you?"

"We're desperately dry," Jonah assured her, smile broadening. "Two pints of ale, please?" He pulled out coins as he spoke, and the woman relaxed slightly and went to serve them. Jonah chatted to her as she drew the beer, rattling on about trivialities with his usual fluency, and she agreed that yes, she could do them a plate of something.

"We don't cook much," she said. "Not much call for it."

"Not a lot of passing trade?" Ben asked, after a long and welcome pull at his beer.

She gave a short laugh. "Here? No."

Ben wanted to ask how they kept going and decided it would be tactless. A girl, about seventeen, with the same strong cheekbones as the landlady but softened by youth, came in with a pile of logs that seemed too heavy for her.

"It's the upkeep," the landlady said with a sigh. "This is a big place. It used to be a coaching inn, but the railways." She spoke as if that were all the explanation needed.

"Do you take travellers still?" Jonah asked. "We're exhausted. Oh, and I don't know if we might need to leave early, so could I pay you now?"

The ready cash was obviously a reassurance, to the landlady if not to Ben, but she grimaced, looking from one to the other. "We've only the one room fit for use, and that's a big bed. It does very well for two if you don't mind doubling up. It's old-fashioned ways, I know, but it keeps you warm."

"That will do very well," Jonah assured her. "Honestly, that will be marvellous. Now, don't fuss, Ben, I'm sure we'll be quite comfortable."

Ben opened his mouth at that baseless accusation and shut it as he realised what Jonah was doing. The idea of sharing a bed with Jonah was—many things, too much to consider now. But it was the landlady's suggestion, in the common way of these old inns, and nobody could possibly question it.

Not that anything would happen. Absolutely not.

"Bethany, a warming pan for the bedroom," the landlady ordered her daughter, and turned back to Jonah's chatter.

Ben couldn't listen. He wasn't sure why Jonah seemed to be so interested in her. Maybe it was simply that he was interested in everything, that jackdaw mind of his as quick to seize on anything as to drop it. That wasn't Ben's concern.

He had accompanied Jonah in the dreamlike haze of utter exhaustion that had possessed him ever since Reading bridge. He'd barely been able to consider the present, let alone remember the past or plan the future. Waking up, feeling himself once more, had brought back all the things he hadn't dwelled on for two days, and he rather missed the state of numbness.

They were going to share a bed again. He pushed that tempting thought away. It wouldn't go. But it had to, because it brought their last encounter back to his mind, making him sweat, and not with desire.

He hadn't made himself face that dreadful, shameful night in Runciman's since it had happened. The impossible rescue, the windwalking, yes, but not what he had wanted to do to Jonah. What he had come so close to. What he *had* done, in hatred and anger, to the man who'd loved him all along, no matter how badly things had gone. The thought sickened and shamed him, so much that his mind flinched away from it. The Ben who might have done that thing seemed to be a madman now.

A madman with his face. How could Jonah forgive that? How could Ben?

He had no right to touch Jonah even if he wanted to. That fact allowed him to shove away the question of whether he wanted to.

He sat in silence, drinking his ale and another, eating without tasting, letting Jonah's chatter and the landlady's more taciturn responses wash over him. A few other men came in, and she went off to serve them, leaving Jonah to sit with him in silence. Finally the drinks were finished. Jonah gave an indicative nod, and they moved together to the bedroom that they were to share.

Men shared beds all the time. There was nothing to blush about.

The room was in the back part of the inn, on the ground floor. It was of decent size but very plain. The rough whitewashed stone walls were somewhat yellowed with dust or age, and had a couple of great black iron hasps sticking out of them. A huge dark wood wardrobe loomed in the corner. The floor was stone flags, likely cold in winter, and there was no fire lit in the hearth, but a basin and an earthenware jug of hot water were waiting on the night stand. Jonah made a noise of intense pleasure, seeing it.

"Thank God, water." He locked the door. "I am desperate to be clean."

So was Ben, after days in the same clothes. He stripped without thought, using the thin towels provided to rub himself all over, until he felt the fug of long travel and fear-sweat lift from his skin. Beside him,

Jonah was doing the same, so much more gracefully, his darkly furred chest glistening with damp, nipples hard in the chill air.

Ben couldn't stop watching.

Jonah didn't seem to notice. He ran the wet cloth under his arms, over his chest, and lower, over his muscular thighs, the nest of black curls. He was half-hard as he rinsed the cloth, wiped it over himself, rinsed it again. His skin shone with damp in the candlelight.

He wasn't looking at Ben. If he had, if he just looked…

Ben stood, helpless, staring. Jonah's body was as compact and muscular as ever. He looked so quick and sleek clothed, so powerful naked. Ben had wrapped his legs over those strong shoulders so often…

No. That was madness.

Ben moved to the big bed. It was a four-poster, evidently once equipped with curtains to pull round and keep the heat in. They had doubtless long rotted away. There was just a pile of quilts and blankets now, sheets warmed by a pan of coals, a bolster, and enough room for two.

Ben crawled in and lay in the bed, facing out.

Jonah blew out the candles and moved round to the other side of the bed, which dipped as he got in. The bed was very cold, except for the almost painfully hot, slightly crispy feel of the linen where the warming pan had rested. Neither of them had a nightshirt—he had a dim recollection of Jonah making some casual remark about lost bags to the landlady. Ben could feel the heat of Jonah's body from here.

It was very dark, and very quiet.

"Ben?"

He could pretend to be asleep. God knew he was tired.

"Ben," Jonah repeated.

"Mmm."

Pause.

"I know it's all gone wrong." Jonah's voice was very quiet. "And I know you probably still hate me—"

"I don't hate you." Ben stared into the dark. "I did, before. When I thought you left me because you didn't love me, or didn't love me enough. I hated you then, but I was wrong, and I am so sorry." His voice shook on the words but it was time and past to say them. "What I did in that bloody place—"

"Don't. It doesn't matter."

"It does." Ben forced the words out. "I wanted to—to hurt you. Me. That's what happened to me, that's what this has done to me. I've become the kind of man who—"

"Who doesn't do bad things, even if he wants to," Jonah came in swift and sharp. "Have you forgotten that? You never had a reason to want to do something horrible to me before. And when you did, it was a good reason, but you *didn't do it*. Look, I know we've done things to each other and, even if you don't hate me…well, it's not like it was any more."

"No." Because what they'd had, that golden idyll, had been a fantasy. Reality lay beside him, flawed and irresponsible and very warm.

"I just wondered," Jonah said. "Could we pretend?"

Ben stilled. He could hear his own deepening breathing. Jonah's tension was palpable. "Pretend?"

"Or forget. Or ignore even, but could we not be a thief and a copper, or two people who did bad things to each other? Just for tonight? Could we just be Ben and Jonah, in the dark? It wouldn't change anything, or mean anything tomorrow. I promise I wouldn't think that it did. But I miss you." Jonah swallowed audibly. "I missed you when you weren't there, and now you are here and I can't touch you and I miss you even more."

"I miss you too," Ben whispered.

Jonah's body was quivering with readiness, Ben could feel it, but he didn't reach out, and Ben realised he was waiting. Letting Ben make the choice. Letting him decide if he wanted to be sucked back into the maelstrom that tore his existence apart, over and over.

Naturally Jonah would think this was a good idea. He lived in the moment, never looking ahead. Ben could see consequences looming on every side, and most of them were terrible.

They should split up, that was obvious. It would have been obvious days ago, if Ben had been able to think properly. His mind was clear now, and he could see it all. Jonah would never change, would never be responsible, quite blatantly intended to steal again should it become necessary. Ben couldn't live like that, waiting for the next disaster, not after Jonah's love had already plunged him into hell. He'd say goodbye tomorrow, and go, before they hurt each other more. It was the only sane thing to do, for both their sakes.

But if this was to be the last night...

He rolled over, under the heavy bedcovers, and reached out, and felt Jonah's whole body twitch as his hand closed on Jonah's shoulder.

"Ben," Jonah whispered, and then he was in Ben's arms, and they were kissing.

Jonah's lips were soft, his beard unfamiliar and prickly, scratching against Ben's own stubble. His tongue met Ben's, sweeping round, tasting of ale and himself. His hands came up, running through Ben's hair, sending shuddering sensation across his skin, and Ben lost himself in being kissed and held and loved.

It was utterly dark in the small room, with its shutters closing out the night. No sight of each other. No sight of the white streak marring Jonah's hair, or the brutal ridge of scarring on Ben's face. No evidence visible of what they'd done to each other and to themselves. It could have been five months ago, when everything was innocent, and Ben let himself believe that it was.

His hands were all over Jonah's skin, remembering by touch, sliding down the muscles of his back, relishing the whisper of the wiry hairs on those strong legs. Jonah gasped in his mouth, tipping his head back, and Ben leaned into the kiss, gripping Jonah's hips, pulling their bodies close together. They both hissed as cock slid along cock.

"God," Jonah whispered, speaking into Ben's mouth rather than breaking the touch. "Will you fuck me?"

"Yes—no. If we leave, uh, evidence—"

"We'll be gone tomorrow." Jonah's hips pressed forward, against Ben's pelvis. "Who cares what they think."

Ben, policeman of a rural town, had a fairly firm idea that leaving sheets stained by illegal acts would be a mistake, of the kind that led to questions, pursuit and amateur justice. He remembered the wild glow in Jonah's eyes, defending him, that sudden sense of how ruthless his laughing lover was under threat. "No," he repeated.

"But I want you," Jonah whined, wriggling up a little.

Ben wrapped his hand around Jonah's solid cock and his own, holding them together, brushing a thumb over both tips and feeling their mutual shudder. "You're going to get me. But we're going to destroy the evidence."

"What?" said Jonah, with some alarm. "Oh, I see. Good plan. One should always have a copper along when committing illegal acts."

Ben rocked against him, curling a slither of dampness over the head of Jonah's cock with his thumb. "God. Jonah." *My Jonah, mine...*

"I want..." Jonah kicked and shoved at the covers to loosen them, making space for movement. Ben rolled him over, pulling him effortlessly on top so Jonah was straddling him.

"Do you do something?" he asked. "Make yourself light?"

"A bit of a boost," Jonah admitted. "Which..." His hands came down, cupping Ben's arse, and pulled, and Ben felt himself lift off the sheets, astonishingly weightless for a second, grinding his groin to Jonah's.

"God!" he yelped as he thumped back down to the mattress.

"I can't keep it up for long. The *power*, I mean. Oh, shut up." Jonah ducked down to kiss the smile off Ben's lips, and they were clutching each other once more, skin to skin, so very hot and close. His tongue was licking inside Ben's mouth, fingers probing, hard arousal driving against Ben's, as though he wanted to possess every inch at once, and it was all Ben could do not to cry out his pleas. The thought of Jonah pushing his legs back, of wrapping his ankles behind Jonah's neck and feeling the man inside him once more...

Not safe, not sane. This wasn't the cottage they'd shared, where the sheets were their own concern. He held on to that thought by his fingernails, and instead pulled Jonah towards him. "Come up here."

"Oh. Oh, Ben, my Benedict." Jonah settled over him so that Ben could run his tongue up his erection. It was sticky-damp and salty already, Jonah always leaked quickly and copiously, and Ben relished that familiar taste, and the familiar sounds. He wished he could see Jonah over him, watch the expression of bewildered, blissful surrender that he knew he wore. Jonah was an active participant in lovemaking, pushing back as strongly as Ben thrust. He had taught Ben there was no real difference between who gave and who took, and until that horrible night at Runciman's, Ben had never felt anything of submission or domination between them, no matter who fucked who. But when he sucked Jonah, it was different. Then the blue eyes glassed over, and his face became naked, helpless, showing him a slave to Ben's mouth.

God, he wished he could see that one last time.

But he could at least hear Jonah's whispers, broken as they were, as Ben took him deep in his mouth, using tongue and fingers, spreading Jonah wide open. "Ben, my Ben, my own. I'll do anything. Oh God, Ben, I swear. Whatever you want. Please. My Ben. Oh God." He was leaking hard now, about to come. There was salt in Ben's mouth, and dampness, and there was salt wet on his face too, as he worked Jonah's erection, because this was unbearable.

Jonah made a noise in his throat and came, filling Ben's mouth. He gagged slightly—it had been a long time—swallowed, kept Jonah there, feeling him, memorising every ridge and vein of him.

Jonah was over him, hands on Ben's shoulders. His breath was close and warm, his hair tickling Ben's forehead. A little splash of damp hit Ben's cheek, where the skin was already sticky-wet. He hoped it was sweat, knew it wasn't.

Jonah was still and quiet for a moment, then he crawled backwards, without a word or a kiss, down Ben's body.

"Don't," Ben said, because he knew bloody well he wasn't hard any more, and he didn't want Jonah to know that.

Jonah crouched there, over him, in unfamiliar silence. His fingers ran very lightly over Ben's thighs.

"Everything I say is wrong." His voice was very low. "Everything I do is wrong. I don't know how to get it right. I think I could, if you told me."

"Jonah…"

Jonah's hands delved, a finger sliding over Ben's balls in the touch that had never yet failed to bring a reaction. He clenched a hand in the sheets.

"I never learned how to do things properly. I don't think. *You* think. You'd have known what to do in autumn, if I'd told you."

Ben would have known nothing of the sort, but he couldn't speak to deny it. Jonah's hands were all over him, probing, stroking, gliding.

"I know I said this wouldn't mean anything."

Lips closed around the head of Ben's cock, bringing him to full attention, moved away again.

"I lied."

Fingers ringing the base of his erection, nesting in the coarse hair.

"I don't deserve another chance. But if you gave me one, I would earn it, Ben. I would. I swear."

"Don't," Ben managed. "Please. Please don't."

"I don't want you to pretend now," Jonah whispered, breath tickling Ben's tight, hot skin. "We both know it's not then any more. I'm not who you thought. I'm the worthless, illiterate fool who lied to you and used you and ruined you and…I want you to let *me* suck you, the person I am. Stupid, stupid me."

Was he asking for forgiveness? Acceptance? Ben didn't know which, didn't know if he could grant either, or if he deserved to. He had no idea what to say, but his hands were in Jonah's tousled hair, pushing his head down, and Jonah gave a moan of pleasure and sucked Ben hard into his mouth.

And Ben did as he had asked. He thought of flawed, lying Jonah, with his assurances of "contract work" and questions about Ben's investigations, and the burglar in the Tring Museum, and that dreadful last kiss in the carriage, Jonah's wet eyes as he left Ben behind. He thought of Jonah running from the law, and flat on the bed in a whorehouse, pretending helplessness to let Ben slake his anger. He thought of all those things as Jonah sucked and licked and served him with mouth alone, fingers gripping Ben's thighs, letting the anger and misery build along with the arousal, a boil to be lanced. He gripped Jonah's hair tighter, pushing his head down, thrusting up into his mouth, but he couldn't force Jonah harder than the man was forcing himself, taking Ben's substantial cock to the root, groaning around it, and when Ben came, it was with a rush of pleasure and pain and love and hate that emptied his soul along with his balls.

He flopped back onto the hard bolster, shaking. Jonah crawled up next to him, and put a tentative hand out, and Ben pulled him into his arms, felt him shudder and held him tight.

CHAPTER TEN

The next morning, he woke alone.

It was a shock to find the bed empty. That was absurd—it was months since he and Jonah had slept together, he should be used to it, but Jonah's scent was around him and for a moment he had believed himself back in the cottage on the lane. The reality thudded into him like a stone weight.

He lay there, breathing, until a thought came that made him jerk upright.

Had Jonah gone?

Surely not. Ben was going to leave, he'd decided that, and last night had made it all the more necessary. Too sweet, too dangerous. He was crawling back into Jonah's web, mindless as any fly, and the fact that the spider intended him no harm didn't make his embrace any safer. So Ben was going to leave.

Ben, not Jonah. *He* couldn't go, couldn't have left without saying goodbye. Surely to God he wouldn't have done that.

Ben was pushing back the bedclothes in a sudden panic, just as the door opened and Jonah came in.

"Morning." He had an earthenware mug in each hand, both steaming. "Tea?"

Ben slumped back against the bolster and the chilly plaster of the wall. "Thanks."

Jonah handed him a mug and came to sit on the bed. He smiled at Ben, but he looked a little nervous. About last night, what had been said in the dark.

Do it. Spenser, you coward, do it.

"Jonah," he said, as Jonah said, "Ben—"

They both smiled, awkwardly.

"You first," Ben said. *Coward. You're just putting it off.*

"Well, what it is, the thing is…I talked to Mrs. Linney." Jonah spoke in a rush. "You know, after last night, with everything she told us—"

"Wait. Who?"

"Mrs. Linney. The landlady? She was telling us about her situation—I *knew* you weren't listening." Jonah gave a theatrical sigh. "She can't afford help to keep this place up, and we don't have anywhere we need to be, and I thought—well, what I suggested was, we could do it. For a couple of days. We can fix things and chop wood or what have you. And she can't pay us, but she can feed us and let us stay here and lend us clothes, she says, and I know it's not money, which we need, but actually, I need a few days of not running. We can always choose a place to go later, we're in no hurry, and nobody will find us here. And I don't know how to do household tasks and mend things, as such, but you do, and you can show me, and I do wish you'd say something. Ben? Was that wrong?" He looked deeply uncertain. "You don't have to— If you don't want to stay, that's all right. But I thought we could work for our keep here—"

"It's not wrong," Ben managed. "It's brilliant. I didn't realise— were you planning this last night?"

"I had an idea," Jonah said, somewhat smugly. "I thought I'd see. And it worked." His face stilled, looking at Ben. "I meant what I said," he went on. "I'm not assuming anything. We'll do whatever you want."

"And the landlady, Mrs. Linney, she's agreed?"

"Yes, although I suspect she'll be watching us like a hawk," Jonah said. "Though I may have, uh, helped her to feel that she can trust us. Just a bit. Well, she can. Neither of us will be pouncing on Bethany, will we?"

"Who's Bethany?"

"The older daughter. There's a smaller one called Agnes."

"Right. Right." Ben didn't give a damn about daughters. All he could see was Jonah, with that open, hopeful look in his eyes, coming up with a proposition of honest work, and a chance for them to rest at last, somewhere safe.

Obviously, he ought to be leaving. He'd decided that. But he needed rest and food and time to recover, and he could always go later.

Mrs. Linney did keep a close eye on them, but she was as good as her word with clothing. She lent them garments belonging to her deceased husband—rough, baggy things a little short on Ben and a little long on Jonah, but serviceable—and took their own clothes off for sorely needed cleaning, and Ben immersed himself in physical tasks. There was plenty to do. The old inn had been deteriorating for years, he guessed, struggling to keep the dwindling clientele who were probably put off by its shabbiness.

He loved working with his hands, though, and was a talented carpenter. Mr. Linney had had a good store of tools, and Ben eyed up the chairs and tables that needed a bit of mending with the pleasant anticipation of something useful to be done. There were days of vital work here, in his estimation, more like months of upkeep.

Jonah was predictably unacquainted with a chisel. He did, however, know what to do with the chickens and the pigs, somewhat to Ben's surprise, and cheerfully obeyed Bethany's orders in the vegetable patch.

By noon, when Mrs. Linney provided an excellent lunch of rabbit pie with a jug of home-brewed ale, Ben was pleasantly conscious of sore muscles and a good morning's work done by both. Flighty Jonah, working. He tried not to let himself believe too hard in that.

"You're a wonderful cook, Mrs. Linney." Jonah swallowed a mouthful of pie. "I haven't eaten so well in weeks."

She accepted the compliment as her due, but made a wry face. "Better cook than landlady. Baking and brewing, that's easy enough. The rest...well, it ain't the employment I'd have chosen."

Ben believed that. She was stern-faced, silent, not a welcoming presence even when she smiled. It didn't create the sort of atmosphere that would drive the men of Pellore up the steep hill, except that this was the only inn for miles. Even so, custom was sparse.

"Why do you run it?" he asked.

"It was Linney's. Now it's mine, and in time it will be my daughters'." She nodded at Bethany, who ate with them. "Linney left us nothing else, and he'd let it go to rack and ruin as it was. Mebbe I should have sold it when he died, but old Linney loved this place, my father-in-law, and I thought I could make something of it, for the girls' sake. Well." Her weather-marked face was lined with weariness, and Ben, watching it, realised with a shock that she was much younger than he'd thought last night, probably less than forty.

"You've done your best, Ma," Bethany put in. "Tain't your fault there's no more'n twenty-four hours in a day. You'd have us working more if there was."

"None of your cheek." Mrs. Linney gave her daughter a severe look. "Well, we keep on, and it's good to have some help."

"For a meal this good, you may have all the help your heart could wish," Jonah assured her, with his glorious smile.

"Tackle the chimney if you're that grateful," Mrs. Linney retorted, but it was clear she was holding back a smile of her own.

After they had eaten and the women had gone to the kitchen, Ben went to have a look at the chimney. "It must be blocked," he said, squinting fruitlessly up into the dark. "I suppose we could try rods. I'd rather leave it to a sweep, honestly."

Jonah sauntered over to the great hearth. "Let me have a look?"

Ben moved back but Jonah didn't attempt to look up the flue, instead putting his hand on the stone of the chimney, over the black beam of the mantelpiece. His eyes lost focus, the pupils widening.

"What on earth are you doing?"

"Um...there's something—broken. Sticks. A nest, I think. And something dead. Cat?" Jonah mumbled the words to himself, staring at nothing. Ben took a step back, the hairs on his forearms rising. "It's very...solid... Ooh, there you are, that's it— Bollocks."

His eyes snapped back into focus, wide with alarm, just as what seemed like pounds of soot cascaded into the hearth with a soft thump. A black cloud billowed up into the room. Ben leapt back, a picture of disaster forming in his mind—the entire pub coated in soot, the hours of cleaning, Mrs. Linney's fury—but before he could speak, there was a sudden sense of suction, pulling at his skin and hair for a second as air rushed by him, and the dusty cloud curled back on itself.

Ben stared, astonished, as the soot shrank in little eddies under the pressure of an invisible wind, heaping up as a black mound in the fireplace. Jonah's eyes were wide, face still with concentration. His mouth moved without sound, hands making a gentle sweeping gesture, pushing the dust back.

Ben twisted frantically around, convinced that Mrs. Linney would be just over his shoulder. She wasn't, thank God. He grabbed for a chair and sat heavily.

Jonah was still a moment longer, until the soot was all piled in the hearth and the air almost dustless, then turned to him. "Are you all right?"

"No." Ben ducked his head against the sudden dizziness. "You're a magician. Christ almighty. You can do magic."

"Um…yes? You knew that. We walked on air, remember?"

"But…" Ben groped for words. "I didn't know you could do *this*."

"I can do lots of things." Jonah looked puzzled. "I can move things around and apply force to things and so on. It's quite convenient."

"Dustsheets are convenient," Ben said. "You put them around the chimney and they trap the soot. That's convenience. This is *magic*, and you use it to do household tasks?" He had a sudden flash of memory, a small domestic disaster averted by what had at the time seemed a startling feat, Jonah holding a collapsing shelf up by a finger. "Is that how you held that shelf up, when it came off the wall?"

"Well, yes. All the china would have smashed, so I—what? What's wrong with that?"

"You were using magic at home," Ben said. "Around me. And I never saw you do it, and I never knew. How?"

"Because you didn't expect it?" There was a wary look in Jonah's eyes, the expression of a child who knew he was in trouble and wasn't sure why.

"Because you hid something you did every day, in our home. You were lying to me with every breath you took."

"But I had to." Jonah sounded slightly panicky. "How could I have told you that?"

"How could you not? How could you— In our *home*, Jonah." Ben groped for words, unable to convey the depths of the shock. He had come to terms with Jonah's hidden life, but as a thing that had been outside them, quite separate to their charmed existence together. The idea that Jonah had been quietly, secretively using his powers all the time, with Ben blithely unaware, made him feel sick and disoriented.

An awful thought dawned. "Did you—did you ever do that thing, with your voice, to make me believe you?"

"Fluence? No! God, no, I swear to you. Never. I only tried once, in the carriage. I wouldn't."

"What else haven't you told me? What else can you do?"

"I don't know!" Jonah yelped. "I don't understand why this is any different to me windwalking—"

"Sssh!" Ben hissed. Footsteps sounded in the passage, past the door, moved away again. They stared at each other, locked in mutual incomprehension.

"Fine," Ben said at last. "If that's all you have to say about treating me like a fool for months—"

"Ben—"

"—then we'd better start work. You do understand you can't let anyone see you do things like that?"

"I am aware of it, yes," Jonah said, voice tight.

Ben grabbed his wrist. "I mean it. People talk in places like this. For all I know they'd burn you at the stake." He paused, horrified not so much by his own words as by Jonah's shrug of agreement: *Obviously.* Ben made himself go on. "But also, if they talk about a magician with a white streak in his hair, suppose word reaches London? The justiciary?"

"Yes, but nobody's seen me, have they? For heaven's sake, I am used to this. Oh, listen—" Jonah reached for him. Ben jerked his hand away, a flinch of pure instinct, because he hadn't forgotten Jonah's hissing words to the policemen on the bridge. *Listen to me…*

Jonah's mouth opened in raw shock. "I was not going to fluence you," he said, low and outraged. "I never have. Don't start treating me like a monster. I've had that all my life. I don't want it from you too."

Ben felt a stab of shame. That wasn't fair. It was surely Jonah in the wrong here. "So stop doing things like—" He gestured at the hearth.

"I *can't.*" Jonah spoke through his teeth. "I am what I am. I can't be anything else. I can't be like everyone else, because I'm *not.*"

"Well, I am," Ben said. "I'm ordinary, and you're—" Extraordinary. Astonishing. Able to walk on the wind and shape men's thoughts and control the air around him, and he had hidden all that power and strength away to live in the cottage with Ben.

Hidden it, or Ben had been, again, wilfully blind to the glaring truth.

That wasn't something he could think of now. He held on to his anger, rather than face Jonah's frustrated misery, or his own complicity.

"Just don't get caught." He rose and turned his back. "And you can explain to Mrs. Linney what happened to her chimney."

Apparently Jonah's explanation was plausible. There were no questions, and that night Mrs. Linney extended the offer of bed and board for another night, should they wish it. They accepted, because it was so much easier than going somewhere else, but that night Ben lay facing away, obstinately refusing to turn and take Jonah in his arms, and Jonah curled on the other side of the mattress in silence.

Ben kept up his silence the next day, knowing it was childish, but raw with hurt and, more, with Jonah's lack of understanding. Apparently he couldn't see the difference that Ben felt as a real and stabbing thing, between what he had done outside their home and inside it. Or perhaps he thought Ben should have realised what it meant to be a magician, a practitioner, at once.

Or perhaps, a wheedling voice suggested, Ben was being a sulky prick when Jonah was trying his best. He couldn't help his nature. And it *was* his nature, that glittering vital spark of joy that made him so glorious to be with, and that Ben's own solid, earthbound, unhappy temperament could extinguish like cold ash on a fire.

Jonah was uncharacteristically silent in response to Ben's quiet, but he plunged into the work without hesitation, chattering away to the girls, leaving Ben on the outside, watching his smiles, wishing they were for himself. There was a lot to be done, and Ben took refuge in that too, relishing the approval in Mrs. Linney's eyes. It seemed a long time since anyone but Jonah had looked at him without pity or contempt.

It was raining the following morning, with one of the abrupt changes of climate that Mrs. Linney assured them were quite usual in Cornwall. She had asked for Ben's help in the huge old kitchen, tackling a problem with the pump handle. It was a two-person job on an ancient bit of machinery with which Ben wasn't familiar. Mrs. Linney was evidently all too accustomed to it.

"Blasted thing," she muttered, wrenching at a nut. Ben put out a hand for the spanner, which she relinquished without protest, sitting back on her heels while he applied his strength. "Makes a change, this. Must be ten year since I had help wi' the brute."

"Mr. Linney's been dead ten years?" Ben asked, and could have kicked himself, because Agnes was very obviously not ten.

Mrs. Linney gave him a look that suggested she was unimpressed with his mathematics. "Four. It's ten years since old Linney, my pa-in-law, passed. Loosen that one, now."

"Right. Mr. Linney didn't deal with this thing, then?"

"Didn't deal wi' much." Mrs. Linney peered at the worn iron. "Arm's slipped, there." They worked in silence for a moment, Ben responding to nods and grunts, till she said, quite abruptly, "It's why we stayed."

"Uh…"

"Here, when Linney passed. He was no good—I've no truck wi' nonsense about speaking ill of the dead. You deserve ill and I'll speak it." She gave Ben a challenging look. He nodded, in full agreement, and she went on, "No good, and my ma told me so, but I was nigh on my Bethy's age and he was handsome before the drink took him. Well." She handed Ben a hammer with an abstracted air. "Ma and I fell out over it, and I married him and moved here. I'm foreign here, see."

"Where are you from?"

"Plymouth," Mrs. Linney said, as one might say, "Far Cathay." Ben, for whom it was all so much Cornwall, nodded wisely. She shot him a sharp glance. "Didn't seem like I could go back wi' tail between my legs. So I stayed here. And you?"

"Me?"

"Aye, you. Where are you from, Ben Spenser?"

"Uh, Hertfordshire. North of London."

"Family?"

That hurt. "Parents," Ben grunted, fixing his attention on the greasy metal shaft he was holding in place. "Brother in the army, in India. Sister married a Scot, moved to Edinburgh." Did they know of his disgrace? His parents would surely not have written to tell them, but if their infrequent letters went unanswered, they would ask...

Mrs. Linney was watching his face. "Travelling folk, eh? Wandering legs?"

"Not me," Ben said, heedless in the grip of regret. "I like being settled." She raised a brow, reasonably enough, since he was here, and Ben managed an unconcerned shrug. "In the long term, I mean. Travelling's not what I'd want for the rest of my life, that's all. Lawrence, my brother, always wanted to cross the seas, see the world, but I'm as happy at home."

"And yon Jonah? He doesn't strike me as the settled sort."

Ben had no idea how to answer that. He had no idea where Jonah's wanderings had taken him before Berkhamsted. More, Jonah had never spoken about his family. Ben had asked once or twice, but Jonah's answers had not been the kind that invited more questions. *We fell out*, he'd said, and since he'd said it with his hand on Ben's cock, it had seemed obvious why.

Ben very much didn't want a conversation about where they were going, or why he and Jonah were travelling together. Apart from anything else, he was sure that Jonah's ready tongue had answered questions already, and that his answers wouldn't match. "Show me how this arm fixes, now?"

They were hard at work in silence punctuated with Mrs. Linney's brusque instructions when Bethany poked her head round the door.

"Ma…"

"Deal with it yourself," Mrs. Linney said without looking up. "Busy."

"But, *Ma*."

A metal arm fell out of place, banging Mrs. Linney's thumb. "Blast it! *Later*, Bethy."

Bethany retreated with an irritated swish of skirts, shutting the heavy oak door with a thump that was close to a slam. Ben thought no more of it. The pump machinery was heavy and intricate but it made satisfactory sense, and he liked Mrs. Linney's definite, unhesitant way of working.

"Good," she said at last. "That'll hold now. Thank you."

"Pleasure. What's next?"

"You've an appetite for work, ain't you?"

"Seems fair. You're feeding us well and it's a comfortable"— *don't say bed, don't say bed*—"room. It's the least we can do."

"Well, there's always more work here," Mrs. Linney said. "Though what I want to know—"

Bethany pushed the door wide. A wave of chatter and laughter rolled into the kitchen with her.

"Just to tell you, Ma," she remarked airily, planting a tray of tankards on the table. "We've had customers in the bar for a good half hour now."

Mrs. Linney shot up from the floor with more haste than grace and headed through to the bar at something close to a run. Ben was close on her heels, cursing himself. They should not have left the place untended, with only a young woman in charge. He hoped the cashbox was still there.

They both stopped at the door, because Jonah was tending the bar.

A group of men filled the seats, unfamiliar faces, travellers escaping the driving rain. Bethany moved among them, serving drinks, face aglow. Jonah leaned on the heavy oak bar as if he owned it, eyes bright, reaching the climax of what was all too obviously an off-colour story.

"…like a rabbit, and *she* said, 'Well, that's what the stick was for.'"

There was an explosion of laughter, ringing off the walls. Hands lifted for more ale. Jonah looked round, still smiling, and caught Mrs. Linney's stunned gaze. He lifted a finger to hold the customers off, strolled over and said, quietly, "They'll all stay for a meal if you can feed them. I'll swear to it."

Mrs. Linney blinked twice and whisked back to the kitchen without a word. Jonah glanced after her, then at Ben. "Well, make yourself useful. How are you at pulling ale?"

Ben didn't know how to do that, nor could he keep up a stream of cheerful banter and ribald stories that persuaded the crowd to stay for just one more, but he could carry trays as well as Bethany could, and his square-shouldered presence was useful when a young man's third mug of strong home-brewed proved too much for him. He had barely got his arm around Bethany's waist when Ben was tapping him on the shoulder with a kind but firm, "None of that, sir." The young man started a protest, took in Ben's uncompromising expression, flushed and let go. Ben moved away, point made, as Jonah chimed in with "Did you hear the one…" to make sure the atmosphere didn't drop off.

"Highest takings in months," Mrs. Linney said that evening, with immense satisfaction. Apparently some of the passing trade had been passing down to Pellore, because there had been a few more faces than usual in the bar that evening, looking with curiosity at the new barman. Ben had to give her credit: once it was apparent that Jonah could pull a pint and count money, and do both with an irresistible cheerfulness that brought responsive smiles even to the leathery faces of the fishermen, she had been quite ready to let him get on. He was, Ben thought with an absurd glow of pride, a natural at it. "Well. I owe you thanks, Jonah Pastern."

"Not at all. I enjoyed it. Better than all that hard work Ben likes."

"The pair of you have more than earned your stay," Mrs. Linney said. "I'm grateful, and I'm shamed not to pay you for all you've done, but—"

"No need." Jonah gave her a boyishly wheedling look. "Although if you could spare me a little time tomorrow…"

"What do you want to do tomorrow?" Ben asked as they retired to the room that night.

"A few things." Jonah must have read his face at the evasion. "I need to go to a shop, for heaven's sake. That's all. I want a razor and some drawers that didn't belong to a dead man, don't you?"

"We don't have any money."

"I've got a bit left. Don't fret."

Easy to say. Ben undressed, carefully not looking at Jonah, and climbed into bed. He was vividly aware of Jonah moving on the other side of the bed. His skin seemed to tingle at the closeness.

"You did well today," he remarked, knowing it sounded abrupt. "Have you done that before?"

"No, but it's not hard."

"I couldn't do it," Ben said. "You're good at it. At people. At charming them."

"I don't think I am," Jonah said. "I don't seem to have much luck charming you."

Ben's eyes snapped wide in the darkness. He had to clear his throat to say, "We both know that's not true."

"It wasn't." Jonah sounded defeated, none of the sparking gaiety there. *I do that to him*, Ben thought. *I make him sad.* "But you see through me now, don't you? All the way to what's inside."

I really don't. "What is inside?" Ben asked.

"Nothing. Nothing at all."

Ben didn't even think. He simply found himself rolling over, pulling Jonah close, inhaling the warm scent of his skin. "That's not true."

"Really?" Jonah didn't sound convinced. "I don't think so. I don't think there's anything there for you. I've lied and stolen and run all my life. I've done more honest work in the last couple of days than in the ten years before. I never thought I could. And I wish I had tried, Ben. I wish I had."

"Sssh." Ben tightened his arm. He wanted to say it was all right, even if it would be a lie. "This isn't bad. We can be here a while longer."

"With you angry with me."

"I'm not." Ben rested his face on Jonah's shoulder blade. "I'm not finding this easy either. I don't know what we do, or how we go on, or if we should. But I'm glad we've had this." He permitted his lips to brush Jonah's skin, very lightly. "It's made things better."

"But it hasn't made them good."

"No." Ben couldn't—shouldn't—argue with that. He rolled onto his back, releasing Jonah. "This isn't the kind of tangle that gets unpicked overnight."

"Are we untangling it?" Jonah sounded urgent. "I need to know, Ben. I'm trying to be what you want, and to make things different, and to live with you not liking me very much, but I don't know how long I can *do* this—"

"I did ten weeks." The words came out without planning, and Ben cursed himself as soon as they were uttered. "Sorry. I'm sorry."

"Don't be." The shift of skin against linen suggested Jonah was hunching up into a ball, a mass of ruffled feathers. "You've every right."

He probably did. That didn't stop him feeling like a swine.

"I shouldn't have said that. I didn't mean it."

"But you did," Jonah said wearily. "Did the time, I mean. And nothing's going to make that go away, is it?"

"I don't know. But I know you're trying and that matters. Come here." He rolled onto his side, tugged at Jonah's tense form, and pulled him closer. Jonah's muscles were rigid, but Ben kept his arm there anyway, not promising anything or offering, just touching him, and they fell asleep like that, in silence, and together.

CHAPTER ELEVEN

The next morning, a Saturday, brought a request from Mrs. Linney that Ben should take a look at one of the parlour chairs. He walked into the room and was instantly caught by the sight that met his eyes: Jonah, by the shelves, and the younger daughter, Agnes, standing on a stool by him. Agnes had been only a flitting presence with a tendency to giggle and run away when she saw Ben, though she'd been out for hours in the garden with Jonah. She was aged about eight, with a mop of blonde curls topping a round face, and right now she and Jonah were looking at the little shelf of cheaply bound books.

"*The Old Curiosity Shop*," Agnes announced, pointing at the volume.

"I know that one too," Jonah said. "Is there *Our Mutual Friend*?"

Agnes peered at the shelves, taking her task with the utmost seriousness. At last she shook her head. "No. That's *The Pickwick Papers*, Ma promised me we'd read that together but she hasn't. And that's *The Life and Adventures of Martin Chuzzlewit*." She sounded out the last word with care. "Why can't you read? *I* can read and I'm eight. I go to school."

"I don't know. I can't learn."

"So how did you read those other books?"

"I didn't, silly." Jonah mock-cuffed her across the head. She giggled. "Ben read them to me."

"Ben's got a frowny face," Agnes observed dispassionately. "Like this." She pulled a scowl.

"He does not," Jonah said, with some indignation. "He never looked like that in his life."

"Yerr, he does so. Like this." She scrunched her nose until she looked like a maddened rabbit.

"More like this," Ben put in from the door. Agnes swung round with her hands to her mouth, saw the terrifying grimace Ben was straining his facial muscles to produce, and shrieked with delighted terror.

"Monster! Monster!"

"Takes one to know one," Jonah told her. "Your mother's calling."

Agnes cocked her head, hearing her name bellowed. She contemplated Ben for a moment, pulled another horrible face with startling suddenness, and fled.

"Frowny." Jonah grinned at him. "Look, Ben, they've Dickens here. I don't suppose... I know we're busy, but maybe on Sunday?"

It was so tempting, and so foolish. Another stone in the reconstruction of what they'd shared. Another link reforged in the chain that bound them.

"We won't be here long enough to finish one," Ben said. He meant it, too. It would be agonising to bring back those blissful days, and dangerous to their fragile peace, and he didn't want his memories tainted any further.

Jonah swallowed, and nodded. "Of course. Sorry."

"I mean, not a novel." Ben couldn't stop himself. He was so tired of pushing away Jonah's efforts, tired of being ungracious, tired of the load of resentment that had come to feel like a burden he wanted nothing more than to put down and abandon forever. It surely could do no harm, he told himself, though he was aware that his resolve had wilted like wet paper at the expression in Jonah's eyes. "But, *Pickwick*'s all bits and pieces as I remember, short stories and episodes. I suppose we could start…"

"On Sunday?" Jonah's eyes lit—he did adore stories—and Ben couldn't stop himself smiling as he nodded.

Jonah vanished shortly afterwards to shop. Mrs. Linney muttered an awful warning about the difficulty of finding a carter to take him to Looe. "He'll walk," Ben assured her, since it was a half-truth, hoping Jonah had the sense to be discreet in his movements.

Ben spent a satisfactory day on repairs, tightening loose hinges and mending joints. He was sweaty and hot by the time he retired to the bedroom with a pitcher of water to scrub off the sawdust, and he was stripped to the waist and rubbing himself down when Jonah came in.

"There's a sight for sore eyes," Jonah remarked.

"If you mean you want a wash…"

"I didn't, no." Jonah flashed him a smile and put a large brown-paper parcel on the bed. "Don't let me interrupt you."

Ben took that at face value, running the washcloth over himself, relishing the feel of the water, and the awareness of Jonah's gaze on him as he sat on the bed, opening the parcel in a rustle of paper. Ben took longer than he might have done, ensuring that the back of his neck, where Jonah had loved to run his tongue and make Ben shudder with pleasure, was very clean. At last he turned to reach for a shirt.

"What the…"

Jonah was watching him with a glazed expression, suggesting that he also remembered his attention to the back of Ben's neck, but Ben was caught by the pile of goods on the bed. There was a lot there. Two horn-handled straight razors, two small piles of clothing—drawers, socks, a shirt. What looked like a couple of papers of sweetmeats. A battered copy of *Our Mutual Friend*.

"I thought we could take it with us," Jonah said. "So if we wanted to read it… What is it?"

Do not raise your voice, Ben told himself. *Do not accuse. Everything he's said, everything he's done. Give him a chance to show it wasn't lies.*

It was all lies, always, said another part of him. *He was handling the money. All that temptation. You let him.* The bands tightened round his heart with the thought.

"Where did you get the money?" he asked as neutrally as possible.

Jonah took a deep breath. "You mean, did I steal it?"

"No. I mean, where did you get it? That's all I mean." He read disbelief and wariness on Jonah's face and went on, forcefully, before any more could be said, "If we can't trust each other, we have to end this now. And I mean that both ways. I have to know you won't steal, or anything else, and you have to know that I believe you won't. If we can't do that, we'll tear each other apart. So tell me, where did you get it?"

"What if I told you I stole it?" Jonah asked, voice thin and tense.

"I don't know. But…" Ben shut his eyes for a second. It felt like stepping off the windowsill once more. "But I'll believe you, whatever you tell me, because you'll tell me the truth." *I will believe. Don't betray me this time. Please.*

Jonah looked down at the bed, at the pile of gifts, and up again, with a tight grin. "I pawned a watch."

"A watch?"

"Which"—Jonah pulled a face and spoke swiftly—"which I *did* steal, granted, but it was *months* ago, back in December. I've been keeping it for a rainy day, but…well, we needed some things, and it doesn't bring back happy memories for me, and I just wanted to get rid of it, to be honest. To *be* honest." He offered Ben a wry smile, and after a moment, Ben returned it.

"I just wanted you to be comfortable," Jonah said.

"I am now." Ben moved over and leaned down, and his mouth found Jonah's for a soft, sweet moment. "Thank you."

Jonah's hand clutched his hair, drawing him closer, just as footsteps clattered along the stone passageway. Ben pulled away, leaving Jonah sitting on the bed, as Agnes burst in without knocking.

"Ma says company's here and where's Jonah?" she announced shrilly.

"I'm here." Jonah rose gracefully. "And this is for you." He handed Agnes one of the bags of sweetmeats. Her eyes opened wide, and she flung herself at Jonah in a hug that caught him off balance and sent him staggering back onto the bed, laughing helplessly.

Then it was a glorious night. The Green Man was full of company, more than Ben had seen there before, or Mrs. Linney had seen in a long time, judging by her reaction. Jonah shone as he drew the ale, that was the only word for it, with a glow of happiness that forced Ben to avoid making eye contact in case they gave themselves away altogether. Half the village seemed to be here, and Jonah was ready with a witty remark for anyone who wanted it, charming them all. Ben, in his shirtsleeves, acted as potboy, clearing the tables of tankards and keeping an eye on who was drinking too much. Mrs. Linney did the same, plus an eye on Bethany, who was mostly ignoring her duties to whisper in the corner with a well-built young man.

"Everything all right?" Ben asked, coming by with a tray of tankards for washing.

"That girl." Mrs. Linney frowned. "Billing and cooing with young Aaron Tapley. A good boy, I dare say, but still a boy, and you know what that means."

"I do," Ben agreed. "But there's no harm to be done while they're in here under everyone's eye."

"Aye. So you make sure they stay there while I wash these, will you?"

That proved to be prescient, as Bethany and Aaron took immediate advantage of her mother's absence to slip out. Ben gave them a couple of minutes, for the sake of youth, before he followed, coming through the door with a meaningful cough that made the young lovers spring apart.

"Just taking the air," Bethany said defiantly.

"Very fresh it is, too," Ben agreed. "Fresher than inside, and a lot darker."

"Did Ma send you to get me in?" Bethany sounded mulish. "I shan't. I'm a grown girl, I can take a turn with my young man if I please and you've no say in it."

"Indeed I don't," Ben agreed. "Carry on." He rested his shoulder blades on the damp wall, giving the impression of a man prepared to play gooseberry forever.

Bethany gave him a puzzled look. "Are you just going to stand there?"

"I'm a grown man," Ben pointed out. "I can stand against a wall if I please and you've no say in it."

Aaron gave a snort of laughter. "'E 'as tha thurr, Bethy." His accent was almost impenetrably thick, unlike Mrs. Linney's. Ben's ear was still adapting to the Cornish speech. "Whyn't ee go in an' us follow drekkly?"

"Drekkly," Ben said. "Does that mean in about twenty minutes, when you think Mrs. Linney is likely to be out of the kitchen?" Aaron's grin suggested that was what he did mean. Ben sighed. "You can have precisely two minutes and then I'll haul you both in by the ears because Jonah needs some help in there. How's that?"

It sufficed. Bethany was not so lost in romance as to ignore the needs of business altogether, and after her two minutes' grace, she set back to work with a will. Aaron looked after her with a fond, if not overbright grin, but it was Ben he came to some half an hour later.

"Bill Penrose there," he whispered, with a clutch on Ben's sleeve. "Bit fuddled, un." He made a "watch out" sort of face. Ben looked in the direction indicated and saw a big man with a face like crumpled hide weaving his way to the bar. Jonah glanced at him, and over at Ben, who shook his head as he began to make his way through the chairs and tables. He noticed that people were edging away from Bill Penrose, holding their drinks protectively.

"Ale." Penrose thumped the blackened oak bar with a hand that was scarcely less tanned with age than the ancient wood.

"I think you've had enough," Ben suggested mildly, coming up behind him, and wasn't surprised to see the big fist clench. He readied himself to dodge, grab and twist, but even as Penrose turned, Jonah's hand had come out to touch his leathery skin.

"Listen to me, you've had enough." Jonah spoke with sublime confidence. "You're tired. It's been a long day for us all, and you'll feel better if you call it a night now and sleep it off."

"Good advice," Ben chimed in, hoping nobody had noticed anything peculiar in that. "You'll feel much the best for a sleep."

"Much better. You don't want any more."

Penrose blinked at Jonah, and sagged back. Ben took his weight in a friendly hold that secured the man's arms. He supposed he should disapprove of Jonah using fluence, but he'd dealt with enough belligerent drunks in his time to take the pragmatic view. "Yes, you come on, sir. Any mate of Mr. Penrose ready to walk him home?"

"Nicely done," said Mrs. Linney after Ben had seen the drunken man off the premises, arm round his more sober brother's shoulders. "He's trouble in his cups, Bill Penrose. Not more'n I can handle, but you and your Jonah did well. Thank'ee."

"Our pleasure," Ben assured her, and did not stop to wonder about "your Jonah" until much later.

CHAPTER TWELVE

They collapsed into bed that night too exhausted for awkwardness, let alone anything more. Ben slept deeply, after a day's work topped by a full evening on his feet, and woke to a steaming mug of tea brandished perilously near his face.

"Awake, sleeping beauty," Jonah said with a grin. "It's Sunday, the inn is shut thank God, and Dora's declared a holiday."

"Dora?"

"Mrs. Linney. She's pleased with us, after last night's takings, and the lack of damaged furniture or deflowered daughters." Jonah's eyes crinkled. "Barman and doorkeeper, who'd have thought it."

Ben sat up and took the mug. "Born to it. When you say holiday…"

"I want to go up the coast." Jonah sat on the bed. "Look at the sea and smell the air and *walk*, Ben." His eyes were wide with anticipation. "I need to stretch my legs. Can we? Will you come?"

A holiday. A day out with Jonah, a walk along the clifftops, so dangerously like those long rambling walks they'd shared last year…

Ben couldn't think of anything he'd rather do.

They set off after a good breakfast. Mrs. Linney—Dora—warned Jonah dryly not to fall off a cliff. Agnes extracted a promise from Ben that he would read *The Pickwick Papers* that evening. Bethany was lost in dreams of her planned meeting with Aaron, to be chaperoned by her mother, but she spared a smiling glance for Ben, obviously appreciating his minor assistance in her romance.

It was a glorious morning, with the Cornish sun, somehow so much brighter than London's, making the heaving sea glitter. Ben watched it with fascination as they walked together over springy turf, scents of salt and thyme and gorse in his nose. Jonah was quivering as he inhaled the sparkling air, nostrils flared, head reared into the wind, and after they had walked for half an hour or so he flung his head and arms back and let out a wild yelp.

"Nettle?" asked Ben, laughing.

"Freedom." Jonah turned on the spot, arms wide, with the unfocussed look that Ben was coming to recognise. He gave a sudden, mad grin, and leapt into the air.

"Jonah!"

Jonah hit the ground lightly. "Nobody about for miles. Just us and the seagulls. And I can feel the wind."

Then he was off, sprinting a few steps, the scent of bruised thyme rising where his feet crushed the plants, and leaping upwards. He spun, impossibly suspended in the air for a second, head tipped back to feel the sun, then dropped, bounded and darted up again. He swung by one hand from the empty air, throwing himself forward and catching on nothing.

Ben only realised his mouth was open when a bee almost flew into it.

He waved the insect away, unable to stop watching Jonah as he played like a puppy, his face transfigured with pure joy. It shivered through Ben, the pure bliss he radiated, the reckless freedom of every movement, and he found he was laughing along with Jonah, standing on the tips of his toes as though he too could dance with the wind.

Jonah looked down, grinned wildly and dropped about ten feet. Ben yelped, instinctively, and found Jonah on the grass before him, flushed with pleasure.

"Want a go?"

"Me?" Jonah gave him a gleeful, conspiratorial nod, and Ben let go of possibility and sense and everything else. "God, yes. What do I do?"

"Anything. Jump. Hands or feet. I'll keep you up." His eyes were blazing blue.

"All right," Ben said, laughing, because it was so absurd, and leapt as Jonah had. His foot met the air, held. He took another step forward, hesitated, and found himself hitting the ground with a jarring thud.

"Sorry, sorry!" Jonah waved his hands. "But you have to keep moving, remember? Keep running or you fall."

"Running," Ben repeated, and launched himself forward and up again.

It wasn't that hard, in fact. He had played scrum half for a tough team and was well used to throwing himself forward without flinching from inevitable impacts. So he ran, and the air held him up, and he ran faster, and turned, because he could, with the wind howling in his ears and whipping away Jonah's calls of encouragement. He climbed, recklessly higher, keeping his eyes on the great expanse of swelling sea, until he was panting, gasping in the wind, and suddenly aware that it seemed a lot more natural to run up through the air than down.

"How do I get to the ground?" he yelled.

"Run down a hill," Jonah called back. "Or drop and swing." He raised his arms in illustration, as if swinging from an overhead bar, and Ben thought, with dizzy lightness, *Sod it*, and did just that.

He dropped. Grabbed with his hands, was held for a second, dropped again, closed his hands on empty air that held him, dropped a third time and fell with jolting shock into Jonah's open arms, tipping him over so that they were sprawled on the turf together, laughing and gasping.

"God," Ben said finally. "God. That was incredible." He couldn't stop grinning. It didn't look as though Jonah could either.

"Did you like it?" That must have been obvious, but Jonah's face was radiating eagerness and the innocent vanity of knowing he'd pleased Ben, and Ben didn't even consider his answer. He simply pulled Jonah over and kissed him.

Jonah's mouth met his, still curved in that unstoppable smile. A memory flashed into Ben's mind, a ridiculous play-fight from long ago—*Stop laughing when I kiss you!*—that had ended with them both so weak with laughter that they'd given up on the attempt to fuck. A bubble of remembered hilarity rose in his chest at the thought. Jonah pulled his mouth away to look at him, eyes wide with delight, fisted both hands in Ben's jacket and yanked him down again.

After a few frantic moments that somehow got Ben's hand trapped under Jonah's back, and Jonah's hands up inside Ben's shirt, Jonah jerked his head sideways so they broke apart, gasping for breath.

"Ben." Jonah's eyes were on his, with immense satisfaction. "Listen, I want…can I try something? Will you come with me?"

"Yes. What? Where? We're in a field."

"We are now." Jonah squirmed out from under him, in what Ben felt was an unnecessarily provocative way, rose and pulled him up, not letting go of his hand as they stood. They went over to stand at the cliff edge together. A gust of wind whipped at Ben's jacket, and he took a half step back.

"You stay there a moment," Jonah said. "Let me see."

"See?" Ben asked.

"Over the cliff," Jonah explained, and dived off.

It hit Ben right in the heart for a fraction of a shocked second. He remembered to exhale, couldn't quite do it. The wind was too strong here to lean over safely, and he couldn't fly alone, so he knelt at the ridge where gorse tumbled over the edge, inhaling the too-sweet scent, and looked down with caution.

It was an extremely long way. Black rock jagged through the white foam of waves many, many yards below. There was no sign of Jonah.

"Hello?" he called. God, he couldn't have fallen, could he? "Hello? Jonah!"

"Here!" came Jonah's cry from somewhere beneath him. "Hold on... All right, want to come down?"

"*Where?*"

There was no reply for a second, then Jonah came leaping out into Ben's field of vision as though he'd pushed himself away from the cliff face. He scrabbled up, lurched sideways at a gust of wind, and landed on hands and knees on the turf.

"Whew." He grinned up at Ben. "There's a ridge down there, set back. Plenty of room. Perfect. Come and sit with me."

"Uh..." Ben looked out at the sea, the drop.

"It's windy, but jump out as far as you can." Jonah's eyes were the deep shade of the sunlit sea. "Trust me."

This was actually insane. *We could just sit on the ground!* part of Ben's mind cried.

But Jonah made him fly. Jonah danced with the wind. Jonah was looking at him with an expectation that he would join the dance, and Ben might be on a terrifying edge but with Jonah's eyes on him it was impossible to step back.

"Now?" he asked, and it was worth it to see the grin on Jonah's face.

"Let me go first. I'll call." Jonah straightened, took two paces and hurtled off the edge. Ben noted how he did it—*jump out, pretend there's something to land on right there, turn...*

"All right," Jonah's voice came faintly from below.

Ben looked out, over the sea and the sheer drop below. "You must be mad, Spenser," he said aloud, and he was laughing at the thought as he ran two steps and threw himself off a cliff.

He landed hard in the air and pushed himself off right away. *Don't stop, don't stop.* Jonah was seated in a sort of niche in the cliff face, over the precipitous drop, beckoning. Ben ran towards him, and the wind caught him and sent him stumbling sideways. "Jesus," he gasped, and suddenly, far too late, he was afraid.

"Here!" Jonah yelled.

The wind pushed at Ben again. He shoved back, desperate, and pounded towards the cliff face, heart tightening in sudden panic as the solid, precipitous stone wall loomed, but Jonah's arms were out for him. He ran towards those in a choking frenzy of fear and disbelief, and landed on stone, knee first, and Jonah's arms were round him, dragging him to safety.

"Hey. Ben?"

Ben's heart was thumping wildly, but he was on a solid surface, and Jonah was there. He managed a breath. "Fine. Fine."

"Head between your knees. Come on, don't faint."

"I'm not going to faint." Ben took a deep breath, and released what he realised was a death grip on Jonah's forearms. "That was a bit... The cliff is big."

"It is," Jonah agreed, with total seriousness, and Ben exhaled hard. He shuffled backwards—the indentation in the rock meant that the ledge was about three feet deep—rested his back cautiously on the rough stone, and looked out, feeling his heart rate slow.

There was nothing but the sea. They were on—under—a promontory, where the edge of the land jutted out, and if he looked straight ahead, there was nothing. No islands, no cliffs, no land. Just the sea, forever, dotted with the red sails of the fishing fleet against blue, like butterflies in the sky, and then nothing till the horizon.

"How far can you go?"

"It's about thirty miles to France," Jonah said thoughtfully. "I couldn't do that without a rest. If I landed on a ship..."

"You'd startle sailors."

"Perhaps they'd startle me." Jonah gave a waggle of his eyebrows that made Ben snort. "No, that's not something I'd want to try. Anyway, I don't want to think about land. I like the endlessness."

"Yes." Ben gazed out. He had his knees pulled to his chest. Jonah had one leg dangling idly over the precipice. "Thank you."

"What for?"

"This. Making me fly."

Jonah looked out at the waves, his face still. He was silent a moment longer, then said, softly, "I've never done it before."

"What?"

"Shared it. Walked anyone else."

"Really?" Ben said. "Hang on. You told me to run to you over a thirty-foot drop. That was the first time you'd done that?" His voice rose on the question.

"Oh, I was sure I could hold you." Jonah spoke with utter confidence. "I windwalk, Ben, I manipulate the ether. I'm really quite good at it. I just never wanted to share it with anyone else till now."

Ben watched a seagull circle by. He should, he supposed, be flattered, but…

"Why not? Why wouldn't you share something so wonderful? Why would you keep that to yourself?"

Jonah shook his head. He was smiling, but there wasn't any humour in it at all, and his gaze was fixed on the horizon.

"Jonah?" Ben felt a shiver of uncertainty at his bleak expression, coupled with the sudden awareness that he was, in fact, trapped on a remote cliff over the sea. "What is it?"

"I was twelve when my powers came in." Jonah's tone was distant. He still didn't look at Ben. "It's a funny thing, you know, the talent. It comes to you, out of nowhere. My family weren't practitioners. I didn't know anyone who was, and nobody knew me, and when my powers came in, they came fast. I didn't know what was happening. I didn't know it was wrong."

"Wrong?"

"I had a God-fearing family, you see." His mouth twisted in a half smile. "I found that I could walk on air—*walk on air*, Ben, it was a miracle. I thought it was a gift from God. I danced through the air to show my parents. My father beat me till the stick broke and then he flung me out of the house. Physically. He took me by the arm and leg and marched me down the path, and threw me outside the gate, in the dust, and spat at me, and said I was no son of his. Changeling, he said. Devil spawn. My mother stood in the doorway and watched.

"So I went away, and I...survived for a while, stole, slept in hedges, all that, and finally the justiciary caught up with me. They were very kind. They assured me none of it was my fault, and everything would be wonderful now, and gave me to a couple of practitioners out in Cambridgeshire for training. Well." He laced his fingers together behind his head. "We very quickly established that I was too stupid to ever learn to read or write, and that I couldn't teach them to windwalk. After that, I was of very specific use to them, cleaning windows and picking fruit, as well as all the other tasks they wouldn't pay a servant for. There was no training, no education, nothing, and there was nobody for me to appeal to. I said, this isn't what you were supposed to do, and they told me to write and complain to the justiciary. Offered to spell the address for me. They laughed about that."

Ben swallowed. It was not easy with the anger closing his throat. He should have known this, somehow. Jonah shouldn't have hidden it. He shouldn't have carried it alone.

"Eventually, when I was sixteen, they gave me a paper to sign. I made my mark, and they told me I owed them for their generosity in food and board, and the accumulated interest, and I'd just agreed to work for them for life to pay for it. They said I'd signed the indentures of a slave."

"There is no possibility that's legal," Ben said. "None."

"Bollocks to legal. I got up that night and stole everything that wasn't nailed down. Then I took all the papers I could find, piled them in the middle of the room and set it on fire."

"You…"

"Where did I go after that, Birmingham? Northampton? I forget. I found a wonderful old lady in Manchester, Auntie Dot. She knew what she had in me, but she gave me fair exchange. She taught me how to pick locks and open windows, how to fence goods, and she never tried to cage me. She said she'd treat me well if I'd treat her well, and we both believed it. She was using me, but we liked each other and it was good. But she was old, and she drank, and she died. Her son took over and told me the agreement had changed. I'd do the jobs he chose from now on. He'd let me do as I wished to indulge his old ma, he said, but it was time to clip my wings. So I ran again. You have to keep running."

An eddy of wind whipped through his piebald hair, ruffling it.

"I tried to find other people after that, but it never worked. They wanted too much. It wasn't enough that I could get in through a high window: the plan would be that everyone else got out safe and I took the risks. *You can fly, you can do it. It's not fair,*" he mimicked. "I had something that everyone else wanted, so nobody ever cared what I wanted. So I decided that I would not be of use to anyone but myself. I tried to keep to that.

"And then I met you. And I stopped running. And I fell."

Ben shut his eyes.

"I should have told you," Jonah said. "You'd have made me stop stealing, and I would have, for you. None of this would have happened. We'd be at home, and you'd have your job, and you'd love me." His voice shook, just a little. "But I didn't tell you, because everyone in my whole life has either hated and feared me for being what I am, or wanted to take it for themselves. I didn't want to see you turn away, or watch you think about how you could use me—"

"*Use* you?" Ben said furiously. "You could have trusted me."

"But I couldn't. That's the point. I was too afraid to trust you, and you paid for it. Nobody's ever cared more about me than about what I can do, and I couldn't bear to find out if you were different. I was afraid to look." He pulled his legs to his chest, mimicking Ben's position, hunched into himself. "Afraid to look, and afraid to have you see me. Contemptible, isn't it? Lying all that time because I knew what you'd think of me."

"You could have stopped stealing by yourself."

"Yes. Except, it never occurred to me that I could. I wish it had. I wish I'd *thought*, but I never think." There was a glistening trail down Jonah's cheek. He swiped at it angrily. "I wish you still loved me."

"Oh, Jesus, Jonah."

"I'm tired of being the villain in the story. I never meant to be, and I don't want to do it any more. I just—God, all I want to do is to be with you. I want to walk the wind with you and come home to our bed. I want you to read to me and play rugby. I want to make you proud of me. I don't need anything else. I don't see why that's so much to ask, that I could just *be* with you. If you loved me. And I want you to love me again. I want that, Ben."

"I can't love you again," Ben said, his heart aching on the words. "How can I, when I never stopped? I couldn't stop loving you when I hated you so much it made me sick to think about you. I used to dream about killing you and wake up crying because I thought you were dead. I can't not love you. I don't know how."

Jonah lunged for him, flinging himself over in a movement of terrifying carelessness that thumped Ben back against the sharp stone edges of the rock face. Then they were kissing as though it was all that stood between them and the precipice. Ben grabbed Jonah's hair, felt Jonah's hands on his shoulder, pulling them close, and kissed, warm and wet and clumsy with need, relishing the scrape of stubble. Jonah was straddling him now, clutching him like a precious thing, and Ben pushed himself up and into his grip, forgetful of the sheer drop and the danger.

"Ben, my Benedict," Jonah panted in his ear, and sat back, on Ben's thighs. "Really mine? Honestly?"

"I don't know how we can do this," Ben said. "But we have to, somehow. God, I've missed you so much."

"I won't leave you again, ever. I promise. I swear it." Jonah's eyes were wide, begging for belief, and Ben pulled him down, and kissed him with all the tenderness that had gone unused and unwanted in the last long, brutal, lonely months.

At last Jonah sighed and sat up. He curved a hand over the side of Ben's face, running the lightest of touches over the scar, and gently rested his forehead against Ben's, breaths mingling.

"What happened?"

He hadn't asked until this moment. Ben wanted to say, *It doesn't matter*, but he owed the truth. "Gaol. Someone went for me with a broken bottle." Shrieking about fucking mollies, fucking coppers, half-mad. The guards had watched them fight, shouting encouragement. "It happens."

"I should never have let it happen," Jonah said softly. "I won't ever let anything happen to you."

"Going to stay out of trouble?" Ben tugged at the lock of white hair, Jonah's own mark of Cain.

"*Yes*. I promise." Jonah's ridiculously expressive eyes clouded, a touch of worry visible. "I mean that. Do you—can you trust me?"

Ben started to laugh. He couldn't help it. The laughter bubbled up, from a spring that he'd thought long dry, until he was shaking with it. Jonah, astride him, gave him a bewildered look. "What?"

"I jumped out of a window on your say-so," Ben managed. "I jumped off a *cliff*."

"Oh. Well. Yes, I suppose that was quite…" Jonah gave a sudden choke. "Actually, don't you think that was a bit rash? You really should be more careful."

Ben doubled over, unable to retort, barely able to breathe. Jonah tipped his head back and gave a whoop of sheer joy that sent seagulls wheeling off with offended croaks. He held on to Ben as the laughing fit subsided, eyes aglow, then shifted to sit next to him and snuggled close.

"I never, ever want to be in trouble for the rest of my life," he said. "I just want to be with you."

Ben leaned over to plant a kiss on his tousled hair. "I love you, Jay."

Jonah's eyes widened at the pet name, so long unused. His unstoppable smile lit his face, and Ben felt the responsive prickle all over his skin. "I love you too."

They watched the sea from their rocky perch for hours, holding hands, kissing sometimes, talking now and then, mostly enjoying the clear air. Jonah had bread and cheese in his bag, and found a spring to drink from after he'd got Ben back up to the clifftop. At last they strolled back from the clifftop, hand in hand until Jonah sniffed the air and warned, "Someone coming."

Ben hadn't thought of lovemaking on a three-foot ledge over a precipitous drop, or afterwards, when all he wanted to do was feel Jonah's glowing pleasure in being by his side. But as they approached the Green Man, the thought of the night to come, a shared bed, leapt into his mind, and suddenly his mouth was dry.

"Jay…"

"Long time till night?" Jonah enquired, and there was the same need in his eyes.

In a safe place, they would have gone to bed at once. There was no safe place, though this was as close as Ben felt they'd find in a hurry, so instead they ate. Mrs. Linney—Dora—had put out bread and cold meats for the family, workers included, and when they'd finished Agnes tugged at Ben's sleeve and held out *The Pickwick Papers*.

Ben read to them all in the parlour. He missed Jonah's head resting against his legs, but at least he was curled in a chair opposite,

Jackdaw

listening intently. Dora and Bethany knitted, as Agnes lay on the hearthrug, staring into the fire. It felt stupidly safe, dangerously good.

"Bed," Dora told them all at last. "Lots to be done tomorrow."

"I might have a crack at that roof, see if I can patch it up a little," Jonah said. "The good weather won't last."

"You're right there," Dora said. "Never does."

Ben paced Jonah down the dark corridor to their room, candle in hand. Light flickered on the walls, making their shadows jump. He was breathless with anticipation and nerves, even shy. It felt like their first time, except that had been unquestioningly confident, and this was terrifying.

Jonah bolted the door and turned to him, taking the candlestick. "I want the light. I want to see you."

Ben nodded, numb. He reached out, and Jonah stepped into his arms. His skin tasted of salt from the sea spray still, and his arms were strong and warm, snaking round Ben's neck as he hooked a leg round Ben's hip. Ben grabbed his taut arse, and Jonah hopped up so his legs were wrapped round Ben's waist, surprisingly light for a second, decidedly heavy after that. Ben grunted and hauled him to the bed, crashing down on top of him to Jonah's breathless laugh. Then they were kissing wildly, hands everywhere, fumbling at each other's clothing, kicking off shoes, tangling each other in their efforts, careless of anything but the need for skin.

Jonah's hand was round his cock now, a possessive grip. "Ben, my Ben. You are, aren't you?"

"God help me, yes."

Ben grinned fondly down at the man beneath him. Jonah smiled up. They both said, together, "Will you fuck me?"

"Oh, for—" Ben couldn't help laughing.

"This is one of many problems we wouldn't have if we liked women. Me. Please."

Ben hesitated. He wanted Jonah in him, needed that wonderful sense of completion and claiming that he wasn't sure he'd dare give

145

anyone else, but he had to make amends for that last time. He kissed Jonah's brow. "Have it your way. Is there anything we can use?"

Jonah looked smug. "I may have bought some oil."

"Confident, were you?"

"I'd say hopeful." Jonah squirmed out from under and went to collect a small bottle and a piece of cloth that he threw on the bed. "Here, sheet protection."

"You think of everything."

Jonah glanced round. "I've thought a lot about this."

Ben crouched on the bed, air chilly on his heated skin. Jonah moved to position himself under him. With the candle on the other side of the bed, the telltale white streak in his hair was barely visible. They could have been in the cottage once more. Except that back then Jonah had been a wonderful fantasy. Now he was flawed and struggling and real, and Ben's hands shook as he reached for the oil. "God, Jay, I need you."

"Have me."

They were both silent after that except for hard breathing, and the soft sounds of oiled fingers and kisses, and Jonah's grunts of effort and moans of encouragement as Ben bore down into him, into tight heat and the clasp of muscular thighs round his ribs and Jonah's open, gasping mouth.

Ben had meant to take Jonah carefully, cherishing him with gentle strokes, and he did try for about thirty seconds. But Jonah raised a brow, clamped his legs down on Ben's spine, and shoved forward to meet him, and then it was frantic. Jonah was wrapped round him, using not just his compact muscles but his powers too so that they were both almost lifting off the bed each time he pushed against Ben. Ben clung on, bracing himself, the steadying force to Jonah's abandonment, holding him close as they picked up the rhythm that neither had forgotten, and pulled Jonah's mouth to his when the first familiar shudders of pleasure hit his lover's body. He swallowed Jonah's cries as he came, sticky on Ben's belly, taut with pleasure, and hit his own climax a few seconds later, grunting Jonah's name.

They flopped together on the bed, interlocked and gasping.

"Think that was too loud?" Ben managed after a while. The other bedrooms were upstairs and at the other end of the corridor, and the stone walls were thick, but it wouldn't do to forget discretion.

"Don't care. I love you."

"I love you too, but I like it here."

"We're not staying anywhere we can't fuck," Jonah said firmly, and Ben drifted off to dreamless sleep in full agreement with that sentiment.

CHAPTER THIRTEEN

The next day was hot and dry, perfect to work on the roof. The slipped slates were visible from the ground, and the reason so many of the bedrooms weren't in use, as the frequent coastal storms blew the rain in and soaked the ceilings. Jonah ensured that none of the Linneys were watching, and went up the outside of the building like a squirrel. He took Ben up from one of the top windows, climbing awkwardly through thick ivy.

The roof needed a lot of repair, but there were plenty of tiles that could be fastened back into place, and the mechanics of it were simple enough. Jonah danced down to the ground to bring up hammer and nails, spare slates and, after two hours in the hot sun, a mug of ale. It tasted very good, and so did Jonah's mouth on his afterwards, as they sprawled on the sun-heated roof, out of anyone's sight.

There were days of work needed just on the roof—days more to spend in this safe place outside the world, eating well, sleeping long nights in each other's arms, not thinking of what next. Ben was all too aware there would be a *next*, sooner or later, but he couldn't make himself face it. This was a holiday from thought, from the world, with Jonah.

"We're doing good work," Jonah remarked one night. "Don't you think? Mr. Penrose—Harry, not Bill, you know, the one who fishes with Aaron Tapley—he was saying how much more companionable the Green Man is now. *Like un afore old Linney passed.*" Jonah had developed a creditable Cornish accent. "That's Dora's father-in-law, not her husband. Can't find anyone with a good word for *him*, but apparently his father was a decent enough sort of man, though everyone says Dora brews better ale. What?"

Ben shook his head, grinning. "You were born for a village, weren't you? You always have to know everything."

"I don't," Jonah said indignantly. "I just listen to people, that's all. Anyway, Harry Penrose is a good fellow, very popular, even if his brother can't hold his drink. He's sending lots of custom our way."

"Why would he do that?"

"Oh, because young Aaron wants to marry Bethany," Jonah explained. "He's Harry's nephew by marriage and Harry's got no children of his own. The Tapleys don't have tuppence ha'penny to rub together so Aaron and Harry are fishing all the hours God sends. But if the inn can do well enough for a wedding portion for Bethany—"

Ben nodded along. They had been at the Green Man for over three weeks now, slipping further and deeper into a domestic routine. Jonah darted around the garden playing tag with Agnes, served behind the bar as if born to it, lit up Ben's heart with his smile. Ben settled to work alongside Dora, mending and fixing, fetching and carrying, keeping order as the pub got busier. They talked, too. Dora was a taciturn, self-reliant woman but she'd borne her burdens alone for a long time. She would speak, sometimes, in quiet moments, of her hopes and fears for the girls, of perhaps going to visit her mother one day, occasionally of the unmourned Mr. Linney and their bitter marriage, ended by his drowning after a drunken fall from the quay. Ben found himself wishing he could speak more freely in return.

He enjoyed Bethany's company as well: her hopeful youth, as yet unworn by care, and her simple happiness with Aaron, who would doubtless be ruled with a rod of iron. At one point he'd worried that the presence of two young men under the Green Man's roof might cause gossip—it would have in Berkhamsted—or even trouble. Dora was a widow, after all, and Bethany an impressionable girl, and hopes could arise…

He'd been so wrong about that it was almost unflattering. Bethany, quite happy with her fisherman, clearly ranked Ben with her own mother in age, and Jonah with her little sister. Dora had made it very clear that she'd had enough of marriage, and had no intention of giving up her rights to a man again, let alone allowing her girls' inheritance to pass through her fingers into someone else's pocket. Ben couldn't quite see how anyone could ignore Jonah's vital, animal presence—it was as much as he could do not to watch every graceful movement—but the Linneys seemed to do so effortlessly. And life was simply too hard for the people of Pellore for them to make it more unpleasant than it needed to be. So Jonah and Ben had slipped into place, unremarked, and nobody seemed to question it.

They couldn't be complacent, of course. The easy acceptance would shatter into sharp edges if the truth about them was known, and they'd be lucky to be drummed out of town with only curses. But that would be the case everywhere, and at least here there were the cliffs, and empty spaces, and a bedroom with thick walls.

And meanwhile, they settled in. Ben recognised many of the local faces now and a lot of the names, although not as many as Jonah, who disappeared into the village or neighbouring Looe and Polperro on any pretext, making new friends and picking up gossip at every turn. *Stretching my legs*, he would explain to Dora. Ben just hoped he wouldn't get caught in midair.

In the end, that was not what caught them.

Jonah woke one morning, sitting upright in bed, and saying, "Storm."

"Storm?" Ben couldn't hear a thing outside.

"There's a storm coming." Jonah sniffed. "It's in the air. Here by the evening, if you ask me. I think we should get on the roof. Do what we can about those last leaks."

He headed up to the roof immediately after breakfast, insisting they needed to get an early start. Dora looked after him. "Knows the weather, does he?"

Bethany frowned. "The boats will be out tonight."

"I'd guess Harry Penrose can tell the weather just as well as that Jonah," Dora said dryly. "Storm, indeed."

Ben shrugged. He had no idea if Jonah could predict weather, but he wasn't going to argue. "If there is a storm coming, does anything else need doing outside?"

He and Dora strolled out to assess the exterior. The sun was hot, the air a little close, the wind picking up. Perhaps Jonah was right. Ben looked up at the sound of his lover's voice and saw him, hanging half off the roof exchanging silly remarks with Agnes as she headed down the road towards Looe and school. He leaned out precariously, waving her goodbye, and Dora sucked in a breath.

"He has very good balance," Ben said. "Wonderful head for heights."

"He must do. If he falls off my roof…"

"He won't."

She shook her head, taking a pace back to rest her elbows on the fence. "He's a bucca, that Jonah."

Ben hoped he'd misheard that. "A what?"

"A bucca. Imp, you might say. You're a steady man, Ben Spenser, but your Jonah's a flyaway one if ever there was."

"You could say that," Ben agreed without thinking, and could have cursed himself. "That he's flyaway, I mean. Not—" He stopped himself before he could say *Not mine*, and wondered if that was better or worse than going on.

Dora was watching his face. "I was thinking. You two, working all the hours here, no pay. Ain't right."

"No need to trouble about that. It suits us while it suits you."

"Aye, but at the least I can make you more comfortable. Now there's all those the leaks stopped, and so few in the way of sleeping guests, you'll want another room. Not to stay cramped up together like that."

"No hurry." Ben spoke as casually as he could. "It's comfortable enough for now and there's more urgent things to be done. Jonah, what's up there?" he called.

"Blasted seagulls, that's what," Jonah yelled down. "Trying to open the place to the elements. Can you bring me up a load more nails?"

Ben was aware of Dora's gaze on him, but she didn't add anything more as he went to pick up the box of roofing nails, and after a moment she grunted and went inside, leaving him wondering.

There was too much work to do to fret, as the sky yellowed and the air became heavier. They spent the afternoon on the roof, securing what they could. Jonah was twitching with nervous energy.

"Can you feel it?" Ben asked. "The storm?"

"Can't you?" Jonah's smile was almost manic.

Ben remembered a day back in the cottage, in the eye of the storm that passed overhead. It had been twilight at noon, the thunder on the heels of the lightning, and Jonah had gone for him wordlessly, fucking him with wild intensity over the kitchen table. At the time he'd just thought the man had been cooped up too long by the rain, but he could see that look in Jonah's eyes now.

"Not on this roof, we'll fall through," he said, and saw from his smile that the same memory was in his lover's mind.

The storm finally hit that evening, sweeping in from the sea with terrifying speed. Huge drops of rain were splatting the hot ground when Ben ran to meet Agnes from the carrier's cart that brought her from school. Dora shook her head when Jonah asked about opening. "We'll light the fire but folks'll bide home if they've any sense."

"They should." Jonah's eyes were glittering bright, picking up the turmoil in the skies. "It's a strong one."

There were no customers. The little family huddled in the parlour after supper. Dora looked ever grimmer as the storm showed no sign of abating.

"The boats went out this morning." Bethany was chewing her thumbnail.

"I know, girl. You've told us often enough."

"But, Ma, the *Dainty Jane* went out and she's not back."

"Well, and what should I do about it that Harry Penrose can't?" demanded Dora. "If you want to be a fisherman's wife, you'll have to learn to live with storms."

"What if Aaron gets drownded?" Agnes asked, round-eyed.

Dora's angry rebuke went unheard in a rolling peal of thunder that sounded just overhead. Agnes squealed piercingly. Bethany clapped her hands over her ears, crying, "Be quiet, you goose!"

"Lord above, don't squabble," Dora snapped.

"She's a stupid child!" Bethany shrieked, and the sisters exploded into furious, high-pitched argument.

"Out! The pair of you! Bethany, you're a silly miss, not fit to be married if you can't control your tongue. Agnes, child, get to bed." Dora hurried the younger girl out as her sister fled the room, and sat heavily, wrapping her apron round her hands, cloth cutting into the thin flesh.

"How bad is this?" Ben asked. He'd never seen a storm at sea and had little idea of what one might entail beyond a dimly remembered Bible engraving of Noah's Ark, but Bethany's fear for her lover was contagious, and he could hear the worry in Dora's fear and anger.

"Bad, if the *Dainty Jane* ain't back. They'll have to ride the storm at sea. The tide's almost at its height now, and Pellore harbour's no size for this. Too rocky, too narrow. 'Less they can make it to safer harbour…" She tailed off. The wind whipped around the Green Man, and Ben winced at a crash that he suspected was a slipping slate hitting the flagstones of the path.

Jonah had been twitching and restless. "I'll check the bedrooms," he said. "See if there's leaks."

It was very obviously an excuse to be moving. Dora stared after him. "Bucca," she repeated.

"Just Jonah."

"Aye, well." Thunder shook the building, an improbably deep note, and lightning illuminated the room for a second through the shutters. Dora looked at the blank wall, in the direction of the sea. Her jaw was set and grim.

"I'm sure Aaron will be all right," Ben ventured.

"Oh, are you? And I dare say you know all about it, do you? Know all about storms at sea, and bringing in a boat through a channel that's narrow at the best with the wind up?" She pushed herself to her feet, face reddening. "Must be a wonderful thing, that. Come from Lunnon and you know everything, more than us simple folk down here."

"Dora, for pity's sake, I didn't mean—"

"Well, I'll tell you what I know." Dora was scarlet, her anger lashing out of her, seeking a target. "You and that Jonah turning up here wi' no luggage, nowt but what you stand up in, and you think I couldn't see you were running? Think I can't see for myself what from, or what you two are? Do you think I'm a fool?"

It was, had always been inevitable, and denial would make bad worse. Ben took a deep breath. He was going to say, *We'll be gone tomorrow*, prepared for, *We'll go now*, if he had to—it was only rain, they'd live—but at that moment the door slammed open, banging off the wall. Dora gave a cry of fury, but Bethany was bursting in with eyes wide in her pallid face. "Ma! Listen!"

They all listened. At first Ben heard nothing but the wailing wind, but then he realised there was a metallic note to it, a discordant clanging. Dora's head reared up.

"It's church bells." Bethany grabbed her mother's wrist. "Ma—"

"I heard."

"Please, Ma." Bethany's face was beseeching.

"What is it?" demanded Jonah, coming in behind Bethany.

"Boat in trouble. There's naught we can do, Bethy, you know that."

"But, Ma, if it's the *Dainty Jane*…"

"Bethy, love—" Dora's face was crumpling.

"I'm going." Bethany clenched her fists. "It's the *Dainty Jane*, I know it is. I'm going down to harbour and you shan't stop me." The girl sounded as determined as her mother ever did.

"No. Bethy!" Dora's voice broke on the cry. She grabbed for Bethany's arm but the girl sprinted out of the room, pushing past Jonah. He looked after her, back at Dora. "What is it?"

"The church bells. Ship in trouble." Dora's angry flush had subsided. She looked grey. "There's no boat has a chance coming in in this storm. Francis Drake himself couldn't do it, and surely not Harry Penrose. Oh, Lord, she was there when they pulled her father from the water. I don't want her to watch her Aaron wrecked. Lord, Lord, what will I do?"

Jonah shrugged. "If you can't stop her, I suppose, go with her. Can we be of any use? If they need hands down there, for anything…"

Dora hesitated, then nodded. She didn't look at Ben. "We'll all go. There might be something to do. I'll check that Aggie's asleep. Get oilskins from the hall, there. Bethy, wait for me!"

They staggered down the steep road to the harbour together, fighting the lashing wind at every step. The rain seemed to come from every direction at once, including up from the ground. Ben was soaked within minutes. Trees shrieked and groaned under the strain, and it was too dark to see the road. They passed the church, its arrhythmically clanging bells almost drowned out by the howling gale, and fought their way along to the end of the stone quay, where a group of villagers huddled, watching the sea.

A small boat, its main mast down and red sails in a crumpled heap, rocked violently with the heaving, thundering waves. It was trying to make the channel into the harbour, Ben could see that much, but with only the small front sail up, he had no idea if that would be possible. A glance at the grim faces around him suggested it wasn't.

"Is it—" Bethany shouted, her words whipped away by the gale.

"*Dainty Jane*," someone roared, without looking round, and Bethany's shriek rose high on the wind. "Look!" A figure was moving on the deck, struggling with the foremast. "That's Harry. Where's Aaron?"

"Can they swim for it?" Ben asked aloud, and got a pitying shake of the head from a neighbour. It hadn't seemed likely, with the plunging waves breaking over dark rocks on both sides of the harbour, but he could see no other way. He glanced round at Jonah, who stared out at the sea, eyes wide and strained. Ben wondered if there was something, anything he could do, and dismissed the idea. If Jonah could quell this storm, he would be a god.

A general cry went up. Ben whipped round, just in time to see the figure fall from the deck of the *Dainty Jane*, over the side. A flash of lightning illuminated the scene, freezing everything in place: the boat, rolled at a terrible angle, the waves curled like a great cat's claw to strike, the man hitting the dark thrashing water, flailing.

"Oh, damn," Jonah yelled, as the thunder crashed down. "I have to go, Ben."

Ben turned. Jonah was stripped to his shirtsleeves, lashed by rain, oilskins in a heap at his feet. He had one end of a massive coil of rope seized in both hands. Ben grabbed his arm. "No!"

Jonah wrenched himself free, starting to shout something, but Ben was already reaching for the nearest fisherman with his free hand. George Tapley, Aaron's big, slow older brother. "Tie it round his waist!" he bellowed over the storm, indicating the rope. "You need your hands, Jay!"

"What the—" George began, and both Jonah and Ben roared at him, "Tie the bloody rope!"

"Are you mad?" Dora cried. Her face was wet with rain and tears. "Nobody can swim that."

"He's not going to swim," Ben said. This was it, this was discovery, but it had to be done, and they were caught anyway. Not that Jonah had known that, and Ben felt a wild pride rising in his erratic lover. "Good luck, Jay. Go."

Jonah grinned crazily back, teeth already chattering, eyes blazing unnaturally blue. "I tell you what!" He was shouting to be heard, a whoop in his voice. "This wind! *This* is for *walking*!"

He leapt into the storm.

Dora screamed, long and shrill. It was the only human sound for endless seconds, as everybody saw Jonah jump up from the edge of the harbour. He was thrown wildly sideways by the wind, and scrabbled upwards as if climbing a wall, staggering up till he'd gained a gap of ten feet above the crashing waves, fighting his way to the *Dainty Jane*. The coil of rope was already beginning to run low by the time the babble of incredulity began.

"Help me hold him!" Ben shouted. He thought nobody had heard, then there was a rush of movement, hard competent hands seizing the rope, and Ben's waist. Ben hung on to the thick, sodden rope that tore at his palms, eyes fixed on Jonah as he was whipped around like a kite.

"How the devil—"

"Bucca…"

"'E's made it!"

Jonah was at the *Dainty Jane*'s plunging side. Ben couldn't see the fisherman struggling in the water any longer, but Jonah's form came briefly to rest on the ship's side, peering down for an instant, before he dropped into the sea.

"Oh God." It was Dora, next to Ben, one of the dozen of them gripping the rope, braced and desperately holding on. It was pulled very tight now. "Did he fall? Can he swim?"

"He never falls," Ben said, wishing it were true. "He never falls."

"*Can he swim?*" she shrieked.

"I don't know!" Ben screamed back. They all lurched as the taut rope slackened horribly. "*Jonah!*"

Lightning seared the air bright, and in that second, Jonah erupted from the water, arms out, an angel without wings. He crashed back down, splashed vertically up again, and this time hauled a form up with him. There was a general cry.

"Harry! 'E got Harry! Pull!"

Jonah had looped the rope round Harry, under his arms. He was behind the fisherman, thrashing to keep them both above the waves. The ropemen on the shore pulled furiously, hauling with all their strength in defiance of the sea and waves and gravity.

"'Ware rocks!" someone bellowed, fruitlessly because there was no way it would carry over the storm, but Jonah was already dragging Harry sideways, around, and into the calmer waters.

"Heave! Heave!" A whole crowd on the jetty now, calling, yelling or just gaping.

Their strange cargo lurched towards them, the rope-holders moving down the quay to keep level in an awkwardly coordinated group. Jonah splashed and struggled in the water as he forged forward, pushing and pulling Harry in, and then half a dozen men and women were extending hands to drag the sodden men in to safety. Harry rolled over, gasping. Jonah flopped over the stone after him, retching seawater.

"Jonah." Ben grabbed for him.

"Aaron?" Bethany shoved him out of the way, eyes wide with fear. "Did you see Aaron? Jonah, where's my Aaron?"

Jonah tried to speak and hiccupped up another mouthful of salt water. Bill Penrose pushed a thick green bottle that reeked of raw spirits into his hand. He took two violent gulps, and a deep breath. "On the boat. Not moving. Unconscious. Or—"

"Get him." Bethany's clutching hands closed round Jonah's sodden, shuddering shoulders. "You have to get Aaron!"

And there it was. Jonah stood revealed, and everyone wanted him. "No," Ben said, fiercely. "No, he doesn't. Look at him!"

Bethany looked up, furious, but Jonah flapped a hand for silence. He assessed the bottle, tilted his head back and drained the lot.

"Bloody hell," said Bill.

"Right," Jonah rasped. He turned to gaze at the harbour mouth and the tossing boat. "Let's see."

"Christ," Ben said. "You can't do that again. Can you?"

"Not a chance." Jonah's eyes narrowed. He gave a quick nod and held out a hand to Ben. Ben grasped it and pulled, feeling Jonah's tight clasp, the closest they could come to a public embrace, as he hauled him to his feet. Jonah's grin was barely sane as he stood. "I'll come back, Ben. Promise. Now…watch this."

He leapt, scrabbling up to the roof of the fish-packing shed. Ben stared, along with the others, Bethany gripping his arm now, and they all flinched together as Jonah sprang out, above them, over to the harbour, heading for the *Dainty Jane*.

Ben could only watch, numb except for the icy pain where the rough rope had torn his hands, as the cries of others narrated Jonah's movements.

"The rocks—"

"'E's over 'em. Well over."

"Lord preserve us. What is he?"

"He's made the *Jane*! He's on deck…"

"Aaron!" That was Bethany, Dora and Aaron's mother, all three crying out together, as the boat rocked violently. Jonah grabbed for a slumped, dark shape on the deck to stop him tumbling over the gunwale, Aaron didn't seem to be moving.

"Bad, vurry bad," George Tapley muttered.

"What's he doing?" Dora demanded. "What's he *doing*?"

That was a damned good question. Jonah stood straight now, on the *Dainty Jane*'s deck, legs braced, poised and waiting. Ben had no idea what for.

There was a tiny lull in the wind, as if it was gathering strength, and as the next blast whipped down, Jonah flung his arms wide. A terrible high-pitched note cut through the gale, as if the wind had been suddenly channelled into a tiny space. The watchers on the quay cried out or put their hands to their ears, and the tortured wind screamed, and the *Dainty Jane* leapt forward. It had only the one ragged sail, no steersman, but for just a second the wind seemed to do exactly what the boat needed, and it skidded forward, safely into harbour, veering to the quayside.

There was a roar from the little crowd, triumph and incredulity combined. Bethany was wrapped in her mother's arms, sobbing her relief, Aaron's mother clutching both of them. Ben glanced at them, back at the *Dainty Jane*, now bobbing and directionless, and then at Jonah, who stood, staring forward, swaying slightly.

"What's 'e up to?" asked Bill Penrose. "Hoi! Aleman!"

Jonah stood a second longer. His knees buckled with horrible suddenness and he dropped as though he'd been shot.

"Jonah?" Ben croaked. "Jonah! Get that boat in!"

The fishermen were already at work, hauling the battered boat to the quay and tying her up. Strong hands brought Aaron's limp body to safety, as Ben waited, twitching with impatience, and finally they dragged Jonah out to lie on the stone quay.

His eyes were shut, mouth open, face pallid. Blood leaked from his nose and ears and ran in droplets from his closed eyelids over his cheeks like tears, washed away by the rain. He wasn't moving.

"Jonah?" Ben was kneeling by his side, grabbing his hand. "Are you all right? What did you do, you damned irresponsible idiot? Jay? Oh sweet Jesus, talk to me."

Jonah lay still. Ben felt panic thicken in his throat. He wanted to check Jonah's pulse, but he'd forgotten how, forgotten everything except his lover, unnaturally still, with bleeding eyes. Rain and salt spray lashed his face.

Dora was hovering by him. "We'll get him inside." She sounded too gentle.

"He's fine. He'll be fine. Jonah!" Ben's fingers dug into the hand he held, and at last, wonderfully, Jonah's eyelids flickered and opened. His eyes were filmed with blood, but they focused on Ben, and he managed a half smile.

"Did it," he whispered, and his head lolled back.

Dora shook his shoulder, speaking more harshly. "*Now*. You come up, you great gawk. It's wet out here."

They ended up in the parlour of the Penrose house, along with half the village, it seemed, crowding in. Aaron, head black and sticky with blood, arm hanging at a bad angle, had been taken to his mother's home, Bethany with him. Harry Penrose sat by the fire, wrapped in blankets, as did Jonah on the other side.

Jonah was hunched on himself, his hair in black and white chaos, eyes wide and wary, still a little red. He was sniffing, but the blood had been scrubbed away, and so had his earlier glee. Everyone was watching him. He looked hunted already.

"How are your eyes?" Ben asked.

"Fine. I overdid it, that's all. Tried to do more than I could."

"And it worked." Ben squeezed his shoulder.

"As far as that goes. I'm an idiot, Ben. I didn't even *think* about us. They'll hate me now. We'll have to run again."

"So we'll run." Ben would tell him about Dora later. "You did the right thing."

"I didn't do it because it was right." Jonah wiped away a trickle of seawater that had dripped from his hair. "I like Harry and Aaron, and I didn't want Bethany to be sad. That's all."

"That sounds as right as it can be. And I'm so proud of you I could shout it to the sky."

"Really? Oh. Well." Jonah shot a quick smile up at him, then turned his nervous gaze back to the whispering villagers who crammed into the room and stared at him. "They're still not going to like it."

"Are they not." Ben stood, shoving back his stool with a forceful scrape, hand still on Jonah's shoulder. Every eye turned to him as silence fell.

They were fearful now, but Ben knew about fear in a crowd. It all too quickly became anger, and Jonah was in no shape to defend himself from a mob. That meant it was Ben's job.

"Right," he said, in his most authoritative tone. "Who's got something to say?"

There was a silence, broken at last by Bill Penrose. "So. New aleman flies, do 'e?"

"What is he?" someone demanded, and there was a clamour. *Bucca* stood out from the flying words, and *spirit*, and *witch*. Ben slammed his hand against the wall, loud thumps demanding silence, until everyone looked at him.

"He's not a spirit or a bucca." He kept his other hand on Jonah's shoulder, feeling the tension. "He's not a freak or a demon. He's a man like you, except that he's got a gift."

"Magic," someone said.

"If you like, but what he does is walk on air. He doesn't curse livestock or spoil milk or whatever else you may be thinking, and I won't hear any nonsense about that. That's the first thing. The second thing is, it's *his* talent to use. Nobody else's. So if any man here thinks there's something wrong with Jonah, or if any of you are thinking how you can use him, or if any of you don't want us here, for any reason at all"—he met Dora's eye, challenging—"you say so right now and we'll be gone, as soon as Jonah's slept off saving Harry Penrose's life, and please God Aaron Tapley's too." He wondered what more to say and fell back on the old formula, so often used to a rowdy crowd on the edge. "We aren't here to cause trouble, but I won't have any trouble caused."

"All very well," grunted Bill Penrose into the silence that followed. "Fine words. But I tell you this." He levered himself up, and glowered at his neighbours, calloused hands clenching. "That there bucca saved my brother, and his boy, and what's more the *Dainty Jane*. Anyone got words for 'im, you'll feel my fists."

"I'll give you words," Dora said. "My Agnes told me she saw yon Jonah flying in the sky and I gave her a clout for storytelling. What do I say to her now, Ben Spenser?"

Ben opened his mouth, couldn't think of anything to say to that. "Uh…admit you were wrong?"

"Oh, right," Jonah said from the fireside. "I just do magic. You're asking for a miracle."

Laughter exploded from every throat, powered by relief as much as anything. The villagers surged forward to Jonah, a chorus of marvelling voices raised in questions and astonishment. Harry reached across the hearth, hand out, and at Ben's shove, Jonah took it.

"I dunno about magic." Harry's voice was hoarse. "But I'd not be here now but for 'e."

"Aye." Bill Penrose slapped a hand on his thigh for emphasis. "Good man, yon bucca. An' pulls a good ale too."

Someone tapped Ben's arm and he looked around to see Dora. She opened her mouth, hesitated. Then she gave him a small, rueful smile, and after a moment, Ben smiled back.

CHAPTER FOURTEEN

Ben rested his elbows on the bar of the Green Man, filled with content.

The old inn was spruce and welcoming, fresh and warm with the late June air. Jonah was outside, flying a kite with Agnes, Ben suspected. The children of Pellore were all obsessed with kites now, ever since Jonah had made one for Agnes and rescued it from the church steeple in a spectacular vertical manoeuvre. Ben had told him off for reckless showmanship, but his words had been drowned by the delighted shrieks of children and adults both, and he grinned at the memory now.

He was tending the as-yet-empty bar because Bethany was down in the village, courting. Aaron was back on the repaired *Dainty Jane*, now his broken arm was mended. There would be no wedding for a while yet, after the young fisherman's enforced break in earnings, but the Green Man was doing well enough to make a spring marriage a possibility, and Dora seemed happy with that. She sang, sometimes, surprisingly tuneful. She claimed it was satisfaction at her newfound prosperity. Ben put it down to the joy radiated by Jonah, irresistible Jonah, with his bright eyes and rippling laughter.

The letter he'd written lay folded in their bedroom. It bore no date or return address, and it would only be posted when he could find a carter or carriage going sufficiently far that the postmark could not lead back to them, but it was done. A letter to his parents. Perhaps they'd tear it up; perhaps they'd read it and know he was safe and well, and be glad. He'd never know, and in some ways it didn't matter. All he could do was send them his love, and what they did with it was up to them.

Eight months ago, he'd been doing hard labour in a gaolyard. Four months ago he'd been alone, lost and so bitter the taste of it had choked him. Now...

Now they were safe. There had been no more mention of separate bedrooms. Dora hadn't spoken of him and Jonah since the night of the storm. Ben had no idea what she thought, and didn't care. She had a prosperous inn, free labour and contented daughters. He and Jonah had a safe harbour and a shared bed with no questions asked. Jonah was absurdly happy, bounding over the fields or playing the fool with the girls.

Their peace might be fragile. They would always be on the edge of a precipice, he knew. But for now it felt like home.

The bright rectangle of sun that streamed in through the open door went dark. Ben looked up with his best welcoming smile as two men walked in.

"Afternoon, gentlemen. What can I get you?"

As they entered, no longer silhouetted against the light, Ben could see "gentlemen" was a mistake. It was very definitely "gentleman", and a striking one at that. A blond man, well over six feet tall, with coldly handsome features, impeccably dressed in light grey. He looked as though he'd stepped out of a London season. His companion looked more like he'd stepped out of a London gaol. Several inches shorter, with cropped, grizzled hair and shrewd fighter's eyes, he wore a manservant's respectable black with the air of a saloon-bar brawler. If he hadn't been at the gentleman's side, Ben would have been reaching for the short cudgel that gathered dust under the bar.

"Ale, if you will." The gentleman came to the bar, somewhat to Ben's surprise. He drew the drinks and passed them over.

"There you are, sir. Thirsty weather."

"And a long journey," the gentleman agreed. The words sounded friendly enough, but there was something in their cool cultivated drawl that set Ben's nerves on edge.

The gentleman wrapped a long-fingered hand around the pewter tankard, making it look cheap with the touch. One finger bore a rather striking ring, Ben saw, a gold band set with chips of quartz and onyx to suggest the shape of a magpie in flight. "Obscure little place you have here."

"It's not the biggest, sir, no. Are you on your way through?"

"God, I do hope so." The tall man spoke with casual dismissal that made Ben bristle. "That's not a Cornish accent."

"No, sir, it's not." *Paying customers*, Ben reminded himself. "Hertfordshire, originally."

"And what brings a Hertfordshire man down to these remote lands?" The tall man smiled, not very pleasantly. "Peace and quiet?"

"Getting away from it all," suggested the manservant. His voice was as rough as his appearance, and his light hazel eyes were fixed on Ben.

"I like it here, sir," Ben said. "Decent folk. Anything else I can get you for now?"

"I don't think so, Spenser."

"Right—"

Ben stopped, a cold prickle creeping up his spine. He hadn't given his name and it wasn't on the door, and a memory was coming back to him now, Jonah's voice. *The right noble earl of Crane. Six foot three of money, mouth and cock. And his pet murderer.*

The thought had come to him in a second. He coughed, repeated, "Right, sir," turned to the door as casually as he could, and bolted, with a cry that was almost a scream. "Jonah! Run!"

Someone crashed into him from behind before he'd got halfway through. Ben went down under the attack, but caught himself, kicking out savagely. He wasn't bad in a brawl, used to absorbing punishment on the rugby pitch, and he'd had a lot of practice in gaol. He could stall them long enough to get Jonah away.

He believed that for a fraction of a second, until an elbow jabbed his kidney, agonisingly painful, as a fist thumped into the back of his head. The momentary dizziness left him face down on the ground, arm twisted to breaking point behind his back, with hot breath by his ear.

"This one's for the wife," the manservant said, and slammed Ben's head viciously on the floor.

"For God's sake, Merrick." Lord Crane's voice sounded rather distant through the pain. "Don't kill him till we've done with him. Where's Pastern?"

"Where's fucking Pastern?" Merrick repeated, and twisted Ben's arm harder till he couldn't hold back the harsh gasp.

Crane sighed heavily. "When I said don't kill him, I also meant don't break him too much. And since it sounds like Mrs. Merrick is making her presence felt out there, I suspect she's got the bugger. Get him up."

Merrick dragged Ben to his feet, taking hold of his hair and not loosening the crippling grip on his arm, and pushed him forward, through the back ways of the pub, out to the gardens. Ben blinked in the bright sunshine. His eyes adjusted, and he set his teeth against the despair.

Jonah, on his knees, head pulled back. A wild-haired blonde woman in boy's clothes with blood running from her nose—the justiciar Saint—holding a knife to his throat. Stephen Day, arms folded, face impassive, looking down at him. And Dora, white-faced and appalled, with Agnes cowering behind her skirts.

"Don't hurt them," Ben croaked.

"I'll hurt him as much as I fucking want," Saint told him through her teeth.

"*Language*," Day barked, and immediately held up a hand. "I beg your pardon, Jenny, I forgot."

"I won't have talk like that on my premises," Dora said, trying to keep the shake from her voice. "And I don't know what that young lady's dressed like, and what's going on? Who are you?"

"My name is Day, this is Lord Crane, and Mr. and Mrs. Merrick are in the role of guards. Do you know these men?"

"No, she doesn't," Ben and Jonah said, in chorus.

"Spenser was tending the bar," Lord Crane put in. "So if he's a customer, he's quite a forward one."

"Mmm. It looks to the untutored eye as though you've been hiding fugitives from justice," Day told her. "Which could put you in quite an unpleasant position. Accordingly, madam, I will be giving the orders for the moment, and I recommend that you don't get in my way."

Dora's mouth opened. Ben caught her eye and nodded, as much as he could. *Do it*, he mouthed.

"Right," Crane said. "Congratulations, Stephen, you have your quarry. What, precisely, do you suggest we do with them? It's past six now, thanks to these endless winding Godforsaken roads, and I am not driving through nowhere all night, any more than I'm sitting up watching the Amazing Escaping Gadfly there."

"Fuck you," Jonah said. "Sorry, Dora."

Day ignored him. "I have an idea. Let me have a look around."

Ben and Jonah's own bedroom was chosen. It was, Day said, quite suitable.

"Iron." Day closed the heavy cuff around Ben's wrist. "I'm sure the lock wouldn't detain Pastern long…" His pupils widened suddenly, and Ben felt something crunch in the lock mechanism of the cuffs. Next to him, held by Merrick and Crane, Jonah gave a sharp inhalation. "Right. That won't be coming off without a hacksaw." Day reached to the other cuff, the one around the hasp, to do the same thing. His ring, the mirror image of Crane's magpie ring, glinted bright against the black imprisoning iron.

Ben was cuffed by one wrist to the iron hasp that stuck out of the roughly plastered wall. The chain was long enough that he could sit or lie on the bed, nothing more. Jonah, white-faced in silent fury, was not chained at all.

"Watch this, Jenny." Day had placed four candlesticks around the bed, on the floor. He made a quick gesture, and all four wicks ignited at once. A moment's concentration, then each flame streamed out sideways as if in a fierce draught, before returning to normal. He glanced at Saint, or rather Mrs. Merrick, who gave a quick nod of understanding.

"Right." Day stepped back to assess his work. "Do you understand the situation?"

Jonah's eyes were glowing blue, the sea with a storm coming. "You stunted ginger shit," he hissed, and winced at Crane or Merrick, or both, applying force to his arm.

"I don't," Ben said.

"It's simple enough." Day moved back to the door. "Pastern is remarkably gifted at escape. You are not. So we're holding on to you. Even if Pastern can get you out of that cuff, the candles are set as wards, linked to you. I'll know if you move outside them, and since we're in the next room, if you break them I'll be here long before you can get away. So." He folded his arms. "If Pastern stays around, we will deliver him to the Metropolitan Police, who will doubtless offer a warm welcome, and we'll let you go."

Merrick cleared his throat sharply. Crane held up an authoritative hand.

"I'm sure you can talk to him later, Mr. Merrick," Day said.

"*I'll* talk to him," said Mrs. Merrick.

"However," Day went on. "If Pastern leaves us before we get to London, we'll still have you. We'll give you to the Met instead, and they can try you for perverting the course of justice, resisting arrest, aiding and abetting a fugitive, accessory to murder and, of course, for nearly killing Mrs. Merrick when you knocked her out and dropped her off a roof." His even tone slipped a little on those words, cold anger slicing through like a razor's edge. Ben could feel Merrick watching him, didn't dare meet his eyes. "You won't be as good a burned offering as Pastern, but you will do. So there it is. Enjoy your evening."

He turned. Crane and Merrick, in silent unison, shoved Jonah forward, so hard he tripped and had to catch himself in the air so he didn't fall on the bed. Their gaolers left the room, shutting the door with a click.

"They didn't lock it," Ben said, into the silence they left behind.

"Of course they didn't." Jonah sprang to the cuffs, glowering at whatever damage Day had done to the locks. "They don't have to. Twisted sod. Bloody justiciars. I can't do anything to these, he's mangled the locks, and this is iron, for God's sake. How strong *is* he?" He looked at the candles, reached out a tentative hand and jerked it back. "And I haven't a clue what to do about those wards, I never learned anything about those. Oh hell." Jonah sat on the bed, head in hands. "I'm so sorry." He swallowed hard. "I'm scared."

Ben's chest and lungs were painfully tight. *Not again, not again...*

No, not again. He wouldn't let it happen, the betrayal, the abandonment, Jonah's tearful eyes before he ran. It couldn't happen, because it would break him again, and this time he would not be mended.

"If they take you," he began, and had to cough to clear his throat. "If they take you, they'll hobble you. Won't they?"

Jonah nodded, huddled into himself like a bedraggled bird. "They'll cut me and I won't be able to walk and... Jesus." His hands were clenched in his hair. "They'll take my flight."

Ben took a deep breath. He filled his mind with Jonah, laughing over the cliff edge, sprinting up a church tower for a kite, fighting a storm to save a life. Jonah on the roof across from a brothel room, holding out his hand. *Score me a try.*

Nobody would take that from him. Ben would stop it happening, and it would be his choice to do it.

"Go." He had to shut his eyes, but his voice didn't tremble at all. "Get out. If you run now, you can be miles away before morning. They said that I'll do, they won't follow you. Go on, Jonah."

Jonah lifted his head, turned and stared at Ben. "Are you serious?"

"Go," Ben repeated. "Just—just go."

"You—you actually…" Jonah was stuttering over his words. "You want me to run, while you go back to prison?"

"It won't be that bad," Ben said. "The accessory charge is nonsense."

"I'll tell you what's nonsense." Jonah whipped round so he was crouching on the bed on all fours over Ben, face white, eyes blazing. "You think I'm going to go, and leave you, again, as if—as if all this— Fuck you, Ben Spenser. Go to hell. I'm not leaving this room until that half-pint son of a whore drags me out, so fuck you if you think I'm leaving you, and fuck you twice if you don't believe me, because I don't know what else I can do. I—am—not—leaving—you. I *said*, didn't I?" His eyes were brimming with hurt. "How can you think I'd do that? What do you think I am?"

"Oh God, Jay." The pleasure of those words hurt more than any pain Ben could remember. "I don't—I'm sorry—"

"You should be. What do I have to do to make you see?"

"Jay!" Ben grabbed for him, one arm brought up short by the chain. "Damn it! Jay, come here. *Here.*" He grabbed Jonah's resisting arm and pulled, until Jonah gave way and tumbled forward, into his one-armed grasp. "Sweetheart, I… But listen, they will hobble you, and I can't bear that. I won't let them take that from you. Please go. Please." He meant it now, with everything he had. He could endure anything for this. "It'll be so much easier for me—"

"*No*. It's my fault. It's my turn."

"That's stupid. I'll get a shorter sentence and easier time. I swear, Jay. You can wait for me."

"You wait for me," Jonah said. "I'm not going and you can't make me and we need to stop talking about this because I think I'm going to be sick. Shit, Ben. I'm so scared." He buried his face in Ben's shirt.

Ben kissed the tousled black hair, holding on, inhaling Jonah with every breath. "Jay, my Jay."

"I'm so sorry I've done this to us. I wish I'd done everything differently. Except meeting you. I did that right."

Ben kissed him again. "I love you, Jay, and I *will* do the time for you, and if you won't let me do that then I'll…I'll be waiting at the gates when you come out. I promise."

"Be there." Jonah's hands gripped his forearms. "If I know you'll be there, I'll be fine. I'll probably be running the place by the time I leave, anyway."

"Of course you will." Ben imagined Jonah, in prison, helpless and crippled, his charm and good looks doing him no good at all. His mind flinched from the thought.

There was a tentative knock on the door some half an hour later: Dora, with a tray of food. Ben had Jonah sprawled over him. Neither of them could summon up the energy to move. It was too late for that.

"Well." Dora put the tray down. "I knew as you two was running from summat when you came here wi' no luggage nor a hat to your heads. I thought I knew what that trouble was. Suppose I was wrong."

"Suppose you were," Jonah said, wearily.

"Not that wrong." Ben would not deny Jonah now. "There's just…more to it."

"I see that." Dora folded her arms. "How much trouble are you in?"

"All of it," Jonah said.

"Listen, Dora, Jonah's not a bad man." It mattered to Ben that she should believe that. "He didn't do half of what they say of him."

"Oh, aye? And what about the other half?"

"It doesn't matter any more," Jonah said. "I'm sorry for bringing trouble on you, Dora, but they aren't after you. Just do what Day says, and we'll be gone tomorrow."

Dora glared at him. "You were in my house, Jonah Pastern. With my children. Now, you tell me. What did you do?"

"Stole. I'm—I was—a thief. I stole, and I helped some very bad people do some very unpleasant things because they threatened Ben." Jonah gave a helpless shrug. "I never stole from you, Dora. I haven't stolen a ha'penny since Ben told me to stop."

She sniffed. "Pity he didn't say that earlier, sounds like."

"He didn't know. None of this is his fault." Jonah's smile was a watery shadow of itself. "You didn't make a mistake taking us in, I promise. I wouldn't have let you down. And Ben's never let anyone down in his life."

"I let you down. I should have stopped you, the night of the storm. That's how they tracked us, isn't it? Rumours of a windwalker. If I'd stopped you, Day wouldn't have found you here."

"And Harry Penrose and Aaron Tapley would be dead," Dora said.

"I know." Ben looked up at her. "You shouldn't get in any trouble. You didn't know you were harbouring fugitives—"

"I knew right well," Dora retorted. "It's why I didn't pay you."

"Well, say you didn't know, about anything. We'll say the same. They're not interested in you and—she's not in their jurisdiction, is she, Jonah?"

"Jurisdiction has nothing to do with it," Jonah said. "This is private vengeance. I crossed the wrong people and they're going to cripple me and then gaol me for it. My mistake. They won't touch you, Dora, just do as they say."

Dora's lips tightened. She gave a short nod, turned on her heel and left without a word.

They held each other in silence for much of the night. It was hard to think of anything to say. Eventually Jonah went to lock the door, and undressed as Ben watched, memorising every inch of his compact, firm body, trying to drill the picture into his brain. Jonah came to him naked and helped Ben strip, shoving his shirt and vest over the iron chain since there was no other way to remove them. They kissed wordlessly, soft and hard, in the steady light of the warding candles that didn't seem to burn down at all.

Ben wanted to remember everything. The wiry black hair on Jonah's chest, the smell of his warm skin, the taste of his mouth, the feel of him as he worked his way over Ben's body with tongue and fingers. They didn't talk as Ben wrapped his legs around Jonah's waist and felt the hard press of Jonah's cock breaching him. The sensation was close to unbearable as Jonah moved inside him, almost without pleasure, because all Ben could think about was their parting. It hurt, and he wanted it never to end.

"Ben," Jonah whispered, poised above him. "You'll wait for me."

"Always."

"Nobody else?"

"Never. There never was. Never will be." Ben's free hand tightened on Jonah's hip. "Make this last, Jay. Don't stop."

"Ben. My Ben." Jonah was moving again, filling him, hands in his hair, and like a coward Ben shut his eyes, because as much as he wanted to remember every second of this last time, he didn't want to remember the look on Jonah's face. It helped, in fact. He could concentrate then, on Jonah's weight, the rasp of hairs and play of muscle, the sensation of Jonah in him, possessing him, claiming every part of him as he had done since he first walked into that little pub and stole Ben's breath.

Ben groaned aloud, heedless of noise—too late to care now—and heard Jonah's panting in his ear. They were moving faster, together, gripping hard, fingers marking skin. Ben pushed back, pulling Jonah deep, and felt pleasure stab through him. Jonah burrowed into him, face in his shoulder, Ben's legs clamped round him, and cried out, and they came together, rocking and pulsing against each other, so entwined that it almost felt impossible that they could be pulled apart.

CHAPTER FIFTEEN

When he woke the next morning, Jonah was gone.

Ben sat up in bed, jerking the chain straight and startling himself with the restraint. The candles were still burning, and the bed was empty.

"Jay?" he whispered aloud.

"Here." It came from above, and Ben looked up to see Jonah crunched up on top of the ancient dark wood wardrobe.

"What are you doing?"

"I was awake." Jonah leapt lightly down. "I thought I'd get off the ground one last time." He moved to the bed, to Ben's arms. "I'm scared, Ben."

Ben's arms tightened. "I know."

There was a knock at the door, a rattle of the handle. Jonah stalked over, glowering, and turned the key in the lock without bothering to open it. He threw himself back onto the mattress with an air that reminded Ben just a little of Bethany in a temper.

The door opened, revealing Day and Merrick. They stood in silence for a moment, looking at the two men on the bed, then Day said, "Well." It sounded resigned.

"I did say, sir," Merrick remarked. "Never bet against my lord. Bastard with a bet, that one."

"And intolerable in victory. All right, tell him the good news, I can handle these two." Day gave Jonah a look as Merrick departed. "I can't say I expected to see you here."

"Fuck you. And I hope you lost something *really* valuable."

Day ignored that, waving a hand vaguely at the candles, which went out, and walking over to the iron chain. "Right. I'm going to take this off. Spenser will come with us to London, as surety for Pastern's continued good conduct. Once he's delivered to the Met, you're free to go."

"Free to go where?" Jonah snarled. "We don't live in London. We don't have any money. Are you just going to leave him there?"

Day's hand closed around the iron cuff, which became suddenly warm. He pulled it open. "Get dressed."

Jonah grabbed his shirt off the floor. "Threatening the unskilled to get your way. Using people's decent feelings against them. I'm amazed you and Lady Bruton didn't get on. You're just the bloody same."

"Stop it," Ben said. He'd caught the look in Day's amber eyes at that remark, and it did not bode well for their journey.

Ben's arm was stiff after the long night stretched out, and it took him a little longer than usual to dress. As he was fastening his boots, Jonah hovering resentfully by, there was a rapid knock, and Agnes tripped in.

"Not now, Aggie," Jonah said. "Go to your mother, love."

"Got a message, dun' I?" Agnes was flushed with excitement. "Lord Crane's compulments to Mr. Day and will 'e come to bar wi' prisoners now. That's you." She pointed at Ben and Jonah, turned on her heel and sprinted out with a stifled noise that was close to a giggle. Ben looked down at his boots, so that he didn't have to see the expression on Jonah's face.

"Presumably he thinks this is a social occasion," Day remarked to himself. "All right, let's go. You two first. Don't try my patience."

Ben took a deep breath. "Come on, Jay. I'm with you."

They headed along the passage in silence, boots echoing on the stone-flagged floor. Echoing footsteps had been a feature of Ben's time in cells, and he winced at the sound.

The heavy door to the bar was shut. Jonah pushed it open. They walked in, and stopped dead.

"What—" Day began, pushing them both forward with surprising force. "Ah."

The bar was full. There must have been thirty people there—Dora, Bethany; Aaron Tapley, his mother and his two brothers; Bill and Harry Penrose. There were regulars from the bar, and most of the fishermen, and John Whittle, who played loosehead prop on the Looe team with Ben, and Agnes, hands stuffed in her mouth and vibrating with excitement, standing on a table at the back of the room.

The adults were all armed, with hayforks, gutting knives, boat hooks, a bristling array of heavy, sharp iron, and it was all pointing at a table in the middle of the room, at which Lord Crane, Merrick and Mrs. Merrick were seated. The married couple wore identically grim expressions. Lord Crane looked almost embarrassed.

"Stephen," he said. "I really must apologise."

Day was apparently speechless. He looked around the room, then took a deep breath, and Jonah swung to face him.

"I know you're stronger than me," he said, voice savage. "I have no delusions about that. But I swear to God, you short-arsed swine, if you touch one hair of any of these people's heads, you'll have to kill me first because I won't stop coming after you till you do."

"Get them out of here or we'll find out just how little time that will take." Day's yellow eyes locked with Jonah's blue, and there was something unpleasant building in the air between them, a kind of thick, greasy feeling that prickled on Ben's skin. Jonah took a step back, into a crouching position, his lips pulling into a snarl. Day's face was taut and intent.

"This is my inn." Dora had a cleaver in her powerful hand. "My inn and my men and you ain't welcome here, nor you ain't taking 'em anywhere."

"*Our* men," Bill Penrose grunted. "Bloody incomers. You leave our bucca be." The great blade he held shook slightly, rather too near Mrs. Merrick's face.

"Oi. Fishfucker." Merrick half rose. There was a babble of voices, angry and nervous and excited.

"Stop," Ben said. "Everyone. Stop this!" He shouted the last words to no effect, with a terrible sense of something irretrievable about to go wrong as the tension in the air built. The Pellore folk were frightened and determined, Day and Jonah were bristling like alley cats, poised on the verge of attack with that dreadful unnatural pressure thickening the air around them, the Merricks looked like a riot waiting to begin and Lord Crane…

…was watching, cool grey eyes seeming unworried by the quivering tines of a hay fork held close to his face. He caught Ben's eye and gave him a quizzical look. Then he picked up a teaspoon and began to tap it on the china cup in front of him, for all the world like a man drawing attention to the toastmaster at a dinner.

The steady chinking sound cut through the noise, slowly silencing it. Heads turned, one by one, except for Jonah and Day.

"If I may," Lord Crane said. "Your attention, Pastern, Mr. Day. Or at least, a cessation of the rather tooth-jarring atmosphere you're creating."

The practitioners didn't seem to hear. Jonah was breathing fast, teeth bared and set. Day's hands were spread like talons. The air was electric now, full of immanent power, as though a spark would ignite it. Ben felt rather than heard a high-pitched buzzing in his ears.

"Spenser." Ben glanced over, startled, at the sharp call, and Lord Crane nodded at the practitioners. "Get yours to stand down, will you, before they set this place on fire between them? *Stephen!*" His voice rapped out, unignorable. Day twitched slightly.

"Jonah," Ben said, as firmly as he could. "Stop it. Back away, now. *Stop.*"

There was another long second's tension. Both practitioners straightened, slow and wary, and whatever was in the air dropped away. Quite suddenly, Ben realised that it had been difficult to breathe. He took a gasp of air.

"Thank you," Lord Crane said. "Now. You." He indicated Mrs. Tapley with a long slender finger. "Madam. Why, precisely, are you here?"

"Mrs. Linney said you're taking that Jonah." Mrs. Tapley, like all the rest, was looking distinctly fearful, but she squared her shoulders. "Well, you ain't."

"Because?"

"He saved my son's life! My boy 'ud be drowned and gone—" Aaron nodded in frantic agreement.

"My life too, and my livelihood wi' it," Harry Penrose put in.

"An' us to marry in spring—"

"—best scrum half in years—"

"Our bucca," Bill Penrose, impressive when sober, pronounced with a wave of his knife. "Pellore's bucca. And a damn good aleman."

"Your…what was that?" Lord Crane enquired delicately.

"Imp," Ben said, flushing.

"Obviously." Crane stretched back in his chair, crossing his long legs at the ankles. "Stephen, far be it from me to dictate your course of action…" Day and both Merricks raised their eyes to the ceiling in silent unity. "However, I don't know if you recall a conversation we had, last April."

There was a pause, in which Day looked puzzled, then he said, blankly, "You must be joking."

"No. I'm inclined to regard the array of ironmongery pointing at me as a character witness for Pastern. Although if it's still pointing at me in twenty seconds' time, I shall come to regard it as a personal affront and react accordingly. Or rather, Merrick will do so on my behalf."

"Right up your arse," Merrick added, sotto voce, eyes on Bill Penrose.

"Weapons down, everyone, please," Ben said, loudly. "Now. *Please.*"

Crane nodded graciously as there was a general movement away. "Thank you. Now, I want privacy, and calm. That means clearing this room, everyone, please. You need not fear for your, ah, imp for the moment, we're going to talk. I will have Spenser, Pastern and Mr. Day at this table now, without any further displays from anyone. And I should be most grateful for coffee."

Dora sniffed. "You won't find any here."

"No, I dare say we won't," Crane said, with weary resignation. "Which is one more reason to resolve this business promptly."

<hr>

The bar emptied of defenders, they sat round the table. Jonah's arms were folded, eyes flickering from man to man. Mrs. Merrick watched him, her silver-blue gaze impossible to interpret. Day, Merrick and Crane were mostly scowling at each other.

Crane had demanded a full account of their last months from Ben, to which Day had added, "Only if I can make him tell the truth."

"Rot you," Jonah spat. "He's not a liar and you're not fluencing him."

"Yes, God forfend anyone should use fluence on the unskilled," Crane said. "Do shut up, Pastern."

"I don't mind," Ben said. "We've nothing to hide."

"Let's see." Day put an electric finger on Ben's skin. "Now, listen to me…"

The experience was not unpleasant, compared to other interrogations. Ben felt a certain lightheadedness, nothing more, and an astonishing ease in speech. Lying would have been difficult, he suspected, but he had no need. He found it effortless to recount their flight, and what happened in Reading.

"Right," Day said as Ben concluded his account of the encounter on the bridge. "Did either of you stop to consider how much trouble that caused?"

"I didn't," Ben admitted, with the dizzy frankness of the enchanted. "And I'm sure Jay didn't. Was it a lot?"

Day put a hand over his face. "It was, rather. Go on."

Ben went on, talking about their arrival in Pellore, the inn, the night of the storm.

"You walked in a gale?" Mrs. Merrick interrupted at that point. Jonah gave a one-shouldered shrug of agreement. "And through water?"

"Spenser's just told us that you were attempting to live undiscovered," Crane remarked. "Performing a sea rescue sounds fairly blatant."

Jonah scowled. "Harry Penrose was drowning, and Aaron had taken a knock to his head on a foundering ship. What was I supposed to do? Be discreet and let them drown?"

"You let men die before," Day said.

"There was nothing I could do about that!" Jonah shouted, slamming his hand on the table. "And if *you*—"

"And was there nothing you could do about Lord Crane either?" Day demanded over him, surprisingly loud. "When you decided to experiment with killing him?"

"He can take his chances like the rest of us, and if you'd put aside your bloody superior attitude for five minutes—"

"For God's sake, stop it!" Ben was slightly startled at his own volume.

"Yes." Crane was watching Ben's face, the grey eyes unreadable and rather unnerving. "I've heard—with the greatest respect—enough from both of you. Carry on, Spenser."

"Well, the villagers saw Jonah windwalk and they didn't mind. They think he's some kind of lucky charm or spirit or something, and they don't want him to vanish. They're not gossiping."

"They obviously are, though, aren't they?" Jonah gave a tight smile. "Of course they talked, of course word spread. If I'd let Harry and Aaron drown, Day'd never have found us. Ironic, isn't it? One attempt to do something decent—"

"That would indeed be an irony," Crane put in, "but actually, we traced you through my fob watch."

"What?"

"The extremely expensive watch you stole from me in December. I had a description circulated to pawn shops with a reward for information." He slanted an eyebrow at Jonah. "I did tell you you'd regret stealing from me."

"You did, didn't you?" Jonah shut his eyes. "Well…bugger."

"In fact, nobody has been talking about windwalkers in Cornwall," Day remarked. "No word reached London at all. It seems your neighbours are close-mouthed."

"Or possibly they like him," Crane said. "Go on, Spenser."

"There's not much more to tell. We've stayed here since. We work in the inn. Jonah's learning to sail. I'm playing scrum half for the Looe team. We've friends here. No stealing, no running, no trouble. We just wanted to live quietly, that's all."

There was a silence. Day glanced from Ben to Jonah, then over to Crane with a slight frown. Crane met his eyes with a look of affectionate understanding that made Ben's throat tighten. He wondered if he looked at Jonah so revealingly, and if he would ever dare to be so open.

"I think the question is," Crane observed, "has Pastern developed a conscience?"

"Of course I've got a conscience," Jonah said. "He's sitting right here next to me."

Ben wanted to shake him. "That's not true, Jonah."

"It is. I'm trying to do the right things because you want me to. You know that." Jonah gave Day a mulish look. "I'm not a saint."

"I don't recall suggesting you were," Day said. "Suppose we hadn't found you, Pastern. That you'd had your quiet life with your prosthetic conscience here. What if he'd left?"

"I wouldn't," Ben said.

Day sighed heavily. "Or fell off a cliff?"

"I wouldn't let him," Jonah said. "But if he did, I'd... I don't know. I don't care. It wouldn't matter any more."

"And there's the problem," Day said. "Right. I want to talk to Spenser on his own, and Mrs. Merrick wants to interrogate Pastern about windwalking, so, Jenny, take him outside now, would you? Nothing stupid, please." That appeared to be addressed to both windwalkers.

Jonah gave Ben a quick, worried look. Ben nodded, since he couldn't imagine this would make anything worse.

"Fine," Jonah said. "But you don't do anything stupid either. My cooperation ends if you lay a finger on him."

"Go *away*," Day told him, and Jonah departed with the Merricks, leaving Ben looking from Crane to Day with a distinct sense of being both outnumbered and outgunned.

"Well." Day propped his elbows on the table. "The thing is, I am not impartial here. Not at all. I saw the painter's victims die, and Pastern could have made Lord Crane one of them when he tore that picture. I would be very glad to see him hobbled and gaoled till he's ninety. Come to that, *you* knocked Jenny Saint out and threw her off a roof. She broke her arm and collarbone, not for the first time. I could happily lock the pair of you up for good."

"But..." Crane said helpfully.

"Yes, thank you, Lucien. *But*." Day looked at Ben. "Well, you tell me."

"Tell you what?"

"What I should do." Day's golden eyes were intent. "You claim he's a reformed character. There's a lot of people here who seem to agree. And, as Lord Crane reminded me, I do prefer to see people back on the straight and narrow if it's possible to have them there. I can't say I expected that of Pastern, and I'm not saying I'm convinced. But the fact that you two attacked my student and my"—a fractional hesitation—"friend shouldn't make a difference to my judgement."

"How can it not?" Ben demanded.

"Because that's what judgement is. Now. You know what Pastern did, and you know the law. I say again, as a policeman, what do you think I should do about him?"

"What can you do but arrest him?" Ben asked. "That is, what are the choices?"

"Whatever I want them to be. I've resigned. I'm not a justiciar any more. I'm acting as a private citizen." Day read Ben's face and added, "If you're planning to challenge my authority, don't. You know what my authority is."

"Being stronger than us?" Ben took a deep breath. "That's not right, sir. Not right, and not just."

"No," Day said. "That's practitioners for you. It's why a practitioner who goes bad must be stopped, one way or another. So why don't you tell me what way you'd choose?"

Ben looked between Day and Crane, over at the wall. Somewhere out there Jonah was in the sun and the wind. He should be soaring.

"I can't say…" He cleared his throat. "I can't say you should let him go. Not in the law. I know what he did. There's crime and there's punishment, that's how it works. But—" He looked back at Day, praying for understanding. "But that shouldn't be all. What's the good in the law, in telling people what's wrong, when they never get told what's right, or have a chance to do it?"

Day was watching him, eyes intent. "Go on."

"The law didn't protect Jonah when his parents threw him on the street to starve. The law did nothing when he was left with, with *slavers*, by the justiciary—"

"What?" Day said sharply, and then, "In Cambridgeshire?"

"Yes."

"The Collinses." Day sat back. "Pastern was one of their victims? I see. I…didn't know that." He chewed his lip. "No. It may interest you to know that the Cambridge justiciary did finally catch up with them a few years ago, and that they were not offered mercy. Carry on."

"Someone should have helped him," Ben said. "You take a child, or a man down on his luck, and give him no help, just kicks, and make it so that any way he turns breaks the law, and then tell him he's a criminal. It's not right. That's not how it should be."

"Good Lord," Crane said. "The copper's a Radical."

"I'm not," Ben said, the denial instinctive.

"It wasn't a criticism. I found myself that a brush with the law from the wrong side gives one a much more nuanced appreciation of crime and punishment."

Day sighed. "Do be quiet, Lucien. Spenser, I fail to see how your eloquent defence ties into the fact that Pastern was a professional thief for years, but do continue."

"That's all. I know he's done a lot of bad things, but Jonah's not a bad man. He's not…like other people, but I don't know how many of you practitioners are." Crane's expression suggested he agreed with that. "But he's got a chance now—with honest work to do and people who treat him decently and someone to show him right from wrong—"

"Some might suggest he could have taken up honest work at any time he chose," Day remarked. "Or that the individual is responsible for himself, for his own actions and morals—"

"No. Or—yes, but— For God's sake, I can't manage alone. I need other people so I can be better myself. I need to know who I'm doing the right thing *for*. I need help sometimes. Don't you?"

"He's got you there," Crane said.

"Perhaps. All right, yes. Granted. But… I could be persuaded that Pastern behaving himself, out of sight and out of mind, would be the best outcome for everyone—you, us, the Met and my people. The damage has been done, the wounds are healing, and there's something to be said for letting them scar over. But I need to know he would stay out of sight, because if he causes any more trouble it will rip those wounds back open, and affect a lot more people than just him and you." Day looked at Ben, eyes very golden. "I need an honest answer. I won't repeat it to him. Do you truly believe he's trustworthy?"

"He's done nothing wrong here—" Ben began.

"In three months. Remarkable."

"We only heard of him via the pawn shop," Crane observed. "And we wouldn't even have been in the country to hear that if Mrs. Gold didn't have the gestational period of a pachyderm. I thought those babies would never appear. It was like waiting for the Second Coming."

"For heaven's sake, Lucien!"

"He's done nothing wrong here," Ben repeated, loudly. "I don't believe he will. I trust him, and I'm staying with him. Whether you hobble him, gaol him or leave him alone; here or in Land's End or John o'Groats. I am staying with him, and he is staying with me, and I can't promise he won't do anything reckless ever again, but I trust him to try his best. I'd bet my life on that. I *have* bet my life on it. If you need a stake, or a surety for his good behaviour, or anything else, I stand for him. For God's sake, Mr. Day, give him a chance." Ben knew he was pleading, didn't care. He'd beg on his knees if he had to. "He hasn't had many."

"I can't comment on Spenser's judgement, Stephen," Crane said. "But I would remind you I won my bet this morning."

"And I'll pay up tonight." Day's voice was quite casual but the look he got from Crane in answer made Ben flush. Day caught his expression and gave a little, rather self-conscious shrug.

"Judging by my narrow escape from lockjaw this morning, there are quite a few people placing faith in Pastern," Crane went on, not noticing or, more likely, ignoring that brief connection. "And if you can just bring yourself to join them, there's a ship waiting for us at Plymouth now."

"Thank you, I'm well aware that's your reason— What was that?" Day was on his feet as the distant shriek cut through the air. Ben leapt too, in immediate panic. It was a woman's cry, and he sprinted for the door, praying. *Jonah, Jonah, please, nothing stupid, not now...* He ran through the kitchen, into the garden, came to an abrupt halt as he saw what was happening, and was sent stumbling by Crane's sizeable frame colliding with his back.

Dora leaned on the fence, one hand clutching her heart, mouth open. Merrick was beside her, shaking his head. The windwalkers stood together. Mrs. Merrick's eyes were wide with excitement; Jonah wore a manic grin. And in the air, Agnes was windwalking. The little girl squealed with glee as she hopscotched madly through the sky, ten feet above the lush grass.

"Oh my God, it's another one," Crane said.

"No, that's Pastern doing it." Day gazed up. "Good Lord, he's talented. That's astonishing."

"It's wonderful," Ben said. Agnes shrieked his name, flailing her arms. He waved up and saw her laugh. "You have no idea how wonderful it is."

"Look at that." Dora came over, head tilted back, watching her daughter. "My Agnes, flapping round like a kite. Lord above. That Jonah."

"What if he drops her?" Day asked, and got a look that should have made him curl up like a salted slug.

"If I thought he'd drop her," Dora said, voice pure ice, "then I'd not let him do that with her. Would I?"

"No, ma'am," Day said meekly. "I beg your pardon."

"Right." Dora folded her arms meaningfully. Day glanced up at Crane, who moved smoothly over to speak to her. Day tapped Ben's arm and nodded over at the fence, indicating that Ben should follow as he walked a few steps away from the others.

Day propped himself against a fencepost and leaned back, watching Agnes in silence for a moment. Something relaxed in his face as the child shrieked with joy, the rigid, implacable, professional expression dissolving into an oddly endearing lopsided smile. This was what Day looked like when he wasn't a justiciar, Ben thought, and a tiny, painful hope grew.

"I'm dancing!" Agnes whirled around.

"Keep moving!" Jonah yelled, grinning, and Mrs. Merrick sprang into the air with a whoop that made her husband laugh aloud.

"Incorrigible," Day said to himself. "I'm surrounded by incorrigibles."

"Mr. Day?"

Day glanced over at him, back at Jonah and over at Dora. To Ben's incredulity, she actually seemed to be dimpling under the relentless pressure of Crane's charm. Day caught his expression and gave a little exhalation of amusement. "She'll be putty in his hands, fear not."

"She's nobody's fool," Ben said defensively.

"I'm not suggesting she is. Well, nor am I, come to that." Day shrugged. "I've had occasion to remark, charm's a dangerous thing."

"There should be a law."

Day looked up at him with a quick grin. "There really should. 'Impeding the rational action of others by the use of charm, good looks and irresistibility—'"

"'A sentence not less than six months'," Ben completed. "With hard."

"It's the only hope for we lesser mortals." Day let out a long sigh and stuck his hands in his pockets. "Oh Lord, Spenser. I used to have morals."

Ben knew exactly how that felt. He wondered if Lord Crane might be almost as disruptive as Jonah to a plain man's quiet life. "So did I."

"Don't underrate yourself. You seem to be doing rather a good job bringing Pastern up to your level. Whereas my standards are eroding by the day." The foxlike smile twitched at Day's lips. "Look, I can't clear his record. If he gets picked up by the justiciary, he'll have to take the consequences. But, God help me, I will send a note to London to say that it was a false trail and there's no sign of him in Cornwall. If you make me regret this, I will take it very personally indeed."

Ben swallowed, hard. "We won't. I swear it. Thank you."

"Good luck, Mr. Spenser." Day shot him a quick, shrewd glance. "If I may say so, Pastern is a great deal more fortunate in you than he deserves."

Ben felt himself redden. "No, he isn't."

"He really is. But he knows it, and that's something. Right. I'd say we'll leave you to it but…" Day looked up, in time to see Agnes take a flying leap into Mrs. Merrick's arms, accompanied by a chorus of shrieks from air and ground, and the clear, joyous peal of Jonah's laughter. "Just now, I don't think we'll get Jenny out of here at gunpoint."

"She can't read, you know," Jonah said that night.

"Who, Mrs. Merrick?"

"Mmm. Same as me. The letters dance, she says. Day thinks it's to do with the windwalking somehow."

"Really?"

"So she says. I like her." Jonah lay on his back. He looked half-asleep. Ben wasn't surprised. The two windwalkers had spent the rest of the morning in a clifftop race of astounding recklessness, returning breathless, windswept and on first-name terms. It clearly hadn't crossed Jonah's mind that Merrick might not want his youthful wife swept off by a handsome young man.

It hadn't seemed to concern Merrick in the slightest. He and Crane had propped up the bar for a couple of hours, swapping increasingly unlikely stories of foreign travels amid a growing crowd of fascinated locals, until the windwalkers had returned and the group departed. Ben had given Day his letter to post in Plymouth. He thought he could trust the man to understand its importance.

The night in the Green Man had been riotous, partly with relief and gratitude at Jonah and Ben's escape, partly because Crane had asked that they should buy every man a round on him as what he called, meaninglessly but effectively, "an apology for the misunderstanding", and left enough money to keep half the village drunk for a week. Dora was rationing that, but it had still been something of a party, with Jonah presiding, giddy with release.

At last they had collapsed, exhausted, into bed, where the iron shackle still hung from the hasp behind them.

"Did you apologise for us throwing her off the roof?" Ben asked. "I meant to, but—"

"Oh, she got over that ages ago." Jonah grinned sleepily at the ceiling. "Doesn't hold a grudge, Jenny. Unlike her husband." He waved his hand airily at Ben's forehead, which had an impressive bruise developing from that bang against the floor. "Shame she's going away. Where's Constantinople?"

"Turkey, isn't it? Why?"

"That's where they're going. Paris and then down through…places, I forget, to Constantinople and along whatever the Silk Road is."

Ben had no idea and just hoped it was far away. He rolled over on one side, watching Jonah's face. "Do you want to travel?"

"Me?" Jonah looked startled. "God, no."

"You sounded…"

"No." Jonah rolled over as well, facing him. "I've…I've had adventures. I've done rooftop escapes and lawbreaking and things, and it's horribly uncomfortable, and I'd rather be here. I like it here. I just want to walk the wind, watch you play rugby. Make kites for Agnes and do things, when I can—Florrie Tapley's roof is in a state, you know, I want to have a look at that—and come to bed with you at the end of the day. I've stopped running."

"You fell?"

"I landed." Jonah's smile was springtime, and Ben reached for his hand and held it. "Come walking tomorrow?"

"There's a game in the morning."

"I forgot. I'll come and watch—"

"And we'll go to the cliffs in the afternoon?"

"And come back here at night." Jonah rolled onto Ben's chest, head heavy, breath warm. "Back here every night there is. God, I'm lucky." He yawned hugely. "God, I'm tired."

"So am I." The candle was burning. Ben contemplated raising himself enough to blow it out, and realised that he didn't have to. "Can you snuff the candle?"

The flame winked out. Jonah gave a little sigh in the darkness, and Ben knew he would be asleep in seconds. He put an arm round Jonah, holding him safe, in no hurry to sleep himself, just relishing the pleasure of his Jay free and safe and warm in his arms. He could lie awake all night, feeling that.

It was Ben's last coherent thought as he fell asleep, and dreamed they were above the cliffs, walking the wind together.

Thanks for reading the Charm of Magpies series! Discover a new part of the world with the story of Ned Hall and Crispin Tredarloe, starting in *A Queer Trade*.

A QUEER TRADE

Apprentice magician Crispin Tredarloe returns to London to find his master dead, and his papers sold. Papers with secrets that could spell death. Crispin needs to get them back before anyone finds out what he's been doing, or what his magic can do.

Crispin tracks his quarry down to waste paper dealer Ned Hall. He needs help, and Ned can't resist Crispin's pleading—and appealing—looks. But can the waste-man and the magician prevent a disaster and save Crispin's skin?

A Queer Trade is a short story set in the Charm of Magpies world, and a prequel to the novel *Rag and Bone*.

RAG AND BONE

It's amazing what people throw away...

Crispin Tredarloe never meant to become a warlock. Freed from his treacherous master, he's learning how to use his magical powers the right way. But it's brutally hard work. Not everyone believes he's a reformed character, and the strain is putting unbearable pressure on his secret relationship with waste-man Ned Hall.

Ned's sick of magic. Sick of the trouble it brings, sick of its dangerous grip on Crispin and the miserable look it puts in his eyes, and sick of being afraid that a gentleman magician won't want a street paper-seller forever—or even for much longer.

But something is stirring among London's forgotten discards. An ancient evil is waking up and seeking its freedom. And when wild magic hits the rag-and-bottle shop where Ned lives, a panicking Crispin falls back onto bad habits. The embattled lovers must find a way to work together—or London could go up in flames.

THE CHARM OF MAGPIES SERIES

Series reading order is as follows

A Charm of Magpies (Stephen Day and Lord Crane)
>   The Magpie Lord
>   Interlude with Tattoos (short story)
>   A Case of Possession
>   A Case of Spirits (short story)
>   Flight of Magpies
>   Feast of Stephen (short story)

Each book is published with its companion story. 'The Smuggler and the Warlord', a very short early story of Crane and Merrick in China, is available free on my website at kjcharleswriter.com.

The Charm of Magpies World
>   Jackdaw
>   A Queer Trade (Rag and Bone prequel)
>   Rag and Bone

These are standalone stories with different couples taking place in the same world. *A Queer Trade* is set in the summer of *A Case of Possession*; *Jackdaw* and *Rag and Bone* are both set in the spring following *Flight of Magpies*.

BOOKS BY KJ CHARLES

A Charm of Magpies series
The Magpie Lord
A Case of Possession
Flight of Magpies
Jackdaw
A Queer Trade
Rag and Bone

Society of Gentlemen series
The Ruin of Gabriel Ashleigh
A Fashionable Indulgence
A Seditious Affair
A Gentleman's Position

Sins of the Cities series
An Unseen Attraction
An Unnatural Vice
An Unsuitable Heir

Standalone books
Think of England
The Secret Casebook of Simon Feximal
Wanted, a Gentleman

Green Men
Spectred Isle

ABOUT THE AUTHOR

KJ Charles is a writer and editor. She lives in London with her husband, two kids, a garden with quite enough prickly things, and a cat with murder management issues.

Find her at www.kjcharleswriter.com for book info and blogging, on Twitter @kj_charles for daily timewasting and the odd rant, or in her Facebook group, KJ Charles Chat, for sneak peeks and special extras.

Printed in Great Britain
by Amazon

32163062R00116